Jase had been her husband's best friend.

Allison remembered all the years she'd known him yet kept her distance. Being near Jase had made her feel wild, rebellious and a little too alive.

But, widowed and disillusioned, Allison hadn't felt alive in months now. And a visit to Red Bluff and Jase McGraw had seemed the best way to remedy that.

Yet when the door opened and she saw the tall, broad-shouldered, dark-haired sheriff with his black Stetson and silver star, her pulse sped up. Jase looked like a stranger. A very powerful, virile, sexy stranger...

"Hi," she said weakly. "On the spur of the moment, I decided to take you up on your invitation to come visit sometime."

"I see." His deep voice vibrated through her. He moved a few steps closer. And a slow smile curved his lips. His very sensual lips...

Dear Reader,

You asked for more ROYALLY WED titles and you've got them! For the next four months we've brought back the Stanbury family—first introduced in a short story by Carla Cassidy on our eHarlequin.com Web site. Be sure to check the archives to find Nicholas's story! But don't forget to pick up Stella Bagwell's *The Expectant Princess* and discover the involving story of the disappearance of King Michael.

Other treats this month include Marie Ferrarella's one hundredth title for Silhouette Books! This wonderful, charming and emotional writer shows her trademark warmth and humor in *Rough Around the Edges*. Luckily for all her devoted readers, Marie has at least another hundred plots bubbling in her imagination, and we'll be seeing more from her in many of our Silhouette lines.

Then we've got Karen Rose Smith's *Tall, Dark & True* about a strong, silent sheriff who can't bear to keep quiet about his feelings any longer. And Donna Clayton's heroine asks *Who Will Father My Baby?*—and gets a surprising answer. *No Place Like Home* by Robin Nicholas is a delightful read that reminds us of an all-time favorite movie—I'll let you guess which one! And don't forget first-time author Roxann Delaney's debut title, *Rachel's Rescuer*.

Next month be sure to return for *The Blacksheep Prince's Bride* by Martha Shields, the next of the ROYALLY WED series. Also returning are popular authors Judy Christenberry and Elizabeth August.

Happy reading!

Mary-Theresa Hussey

Mary-Theresa Hussey
Senior Editor

Please address questions and book requests to:
Silhouette Reader Service
U.S.: 3010 Walden Ave., P.O. Box 1325, Buffalo, NY 14269
Canadian: P.O. Box 609, Fort Erie, Ont. L2A 5X3

Tall, Dark & True

KAREN ROSE SMITH

SILHOUETTE *Romance*.

Published by Silhouette Books

America's Publisher of Contemporary Romance

In loving memory of my grandparents,
Antonio and Rosalie Arcuri. Thank you for my first glimpse of a world outside my own. I miss you. Love, Karen

Acknowledgments

Thanks to Dr. Stephen Clancy for his superb answers to my medical questions, and to Karen Templeton and Jeannette Wood, who helped me remember Albuquerque through their eyes.

 SILHOUETTE BOOKS

ISBN 0-373-19506-0

TALL, DARK & TRUE

KAREN ROSE SMITH

caught her first glimpse of New Mexico from a train when she was sixteen and traveling across the country with her grandparents. Back then, she knew she would never forget how blue the sky was or how the red bluffs seemed to touch the clouds. One day she hopes to return to New Mexico, but for now she loves writing full-time in her home in Pennyslvania, where she lives with her husband, Steve, and their cat, Kasie.

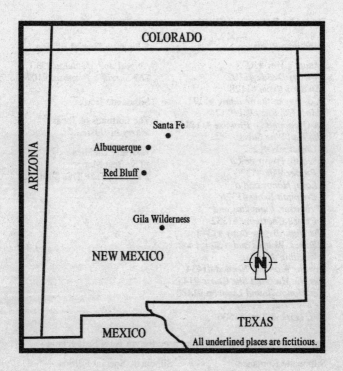

COLORADO

ARIZONA

Santa Fe •

Albuquerque •

Red Bluff •

Gila Wilderness •

NEW MEXICO

MEXICO

TEXAS

All underlined places are fictitious.

Chapter One

Allison Rhodes parked her rental car in the gravel lot beside the Red Bluff sheriff's office, then took two huge deep breaths. Had she lost her mind, flying out here without even telling Jase McGraw she was coming?

The letters she'd found in the closet after her husband's funeral had haunted her over the past year. Two days ago she'd found yet another.

She'd impulsively made the decision to fly to New Mexico. But it had seemed sane. Even more than that. Necessary. She'd needed to get away from everything that had reminded her of her husband's betrayal.

Unfortunately, those letters were indelibly engraved on her mind. They were love letters from Tanya Jacobs—Dave's partner on the Richmond police force. He'd kept them in a shoe box under an old pair of hiking boots. From what she'd read, the affair had been going on for a year and she'd been blind to it. She'd been an absolute fool. Her grief had been muddied by so much anger, so much hurt and so much self-analysis that she couldn't sleep and had lost weight. Then she'd found that last letter—

The June sun beat down on Allison as she climbed out of her car, wiped nervous palms on her white jeans and went around to the front of the sheriff's office. After mounting the two wooden steps, she opened the plate-glass door with a black star painted on it. Inside, a fan hummed, swirling hot air throughout the room.

A woman with startling red curly hair sat at a battered, massive wooden desk. There was a computer along with electronic gizmos and switches beside her, and she looked up at Allison as if strangers were an oddity. Across the small entrance area, on the other side of the room, were two large metal desks with wooden swivel chairs. One of those chairs was filled by a hulking uniformed officer who looked to be involved with paperwork of some kind.

"Can I help you?" the red-haired woman asked.

"I'm looking for Jase McGraw."

That brought the deputy's head up with a wide grin. "You and half of the other women in this county."

"Virgil, hush up," the woman scolded him. "You're just jealous the *Albuquerque Sentinel* didn't name you as most eligible stud last year."

Virgil's face reddened. "You're getting too sassy for a dispatcher," he grumbled.

The dispatcher looked Allison up and down again. "And exactly why do you want to see Sheriff McGraw?"

Allison squared her shoulders but took another deep breath before she answered. "We're old friends."

"And from the sound of it, you're from the same place he came from. Richmond, right?"

"Yes, that's right." Allison decided she wasn't going to give this woman any more information than she had to.

"Well, it's like this," the woman drawled. "The sheriff's out on a call right now."

"A call my—" Virgil stopped. "He's checking out the traffic light down on Rio."

"Like I said," the dispatcher repeated, "he's out on a call. I'll see if I can raise him."

Allison didn't know if she was supposed to stand there and wait, or sit on the hard wooden bench inside the door. Instead of doing either, she went over to the water cooler, extracted a paper cup and filled it. As she sipped at it, she heard the dispatcher call a code, followed by Jase's name.

Then she heard his deep, strong voice flow from the speaker. "What is it, Clara?"

"There's a woman here to see you. She says her name is—"

"Allison Rhodes," Allison filled in for her.

Clara repeated into the mike, "Allison Rhodes."

There was a very long silence, then finally a click. Jase's voice came through loud and clear. "I'll be there in five minutes."

Now Allison did walk over to the bench and sit down, her legs feeling a little shaky. It had been three weeks since she'd seen Jase at his niece's christening. What would he think about her turning up in his office like this?

She'd always been disconcerted by Jase, who'd been her husband's best friend. She'd become friends with his sister Patty because they worked at the same hospital. At the christening she'd heard him telling Patty that the sky in Red Bluff was bluer than blue and that the red cliffs practically touched the clouds. The picture had sounded entrancing and Allison had remarked that she'd like to visit the Southwest sometime. Patty had suggested immediately, "You should go stay with Jase. He has a spare room."

Her brother had looked surprised, but recovered, saying he *did* have a spare room and Allison was welcome anytime. Their gazes had met and Allison had remembered all the years she'd known him yet kept her distance.

Now the thought of being anywhere near Jase Mc-Graw made her feel wild, rebellious and a little bit too alive. She hadn't felt alive in months. Never in her thirty-two years had she done anything as impulsive as this. But then she'd never had the motivation before, either. At this moment she just wanted to forget her life in Richmond. A visit to Red Bluff and Jase McGraw had seemed the best way to do that. If he hadn't really meant his put-on-the-spot invitation, she'd stay in a motel.

The black, round clock on the wall ticked off five minutes, each one of them seeming like an eternity. But then Allison heard the rumble of a vehicle coming down the street and as she looked out through the window, she saw a black SUV with the sheriff's logo in white on the side. Glimpsing the tall, broad-shouldered, dark-haired man inside, her pulse sped up.

She drank the last of the water, crumpled the cup and threw it into the trash can.

The door to the sheriff's office opened and Jase came striding inside. His hand went to the brim of his black Stetson and he doffed it, holding it by his side as he stared at her.

Allison had seen Jase in uniform before, but city blues, not a Southwest sheriff's uniform. There was a silver star pinned on his slate-gray Western-cut shirt. Slate-gray slacks with black stripes down the sides made him look taller than the six foot two that he was. With his black boots and black bolo tie held at the collar by a New Mexico state emblem, he almost looked like a stranger. A very powerful, virile, sexy stranger.

"Hi," she said, making a weak attempt at a smile. "I decided to take you up on your invitation."

His brandy-colored eyes were potently appraising as they drifted from her shoulder-length blond hair, down her white-and-pink-striped knit top and white jeans to the sandals on her feet. "I see you have."

His voice seemed to vibrate through her. She told herself she was just tired and unsettled and unsure. "I took you at your word, but if that's a problem, I can stay in a motel. In fact, I can drive back to Albuquerque and—"

"Whoa. You're not driving back to Albuquerque. When I make an offer, I mean it. I'm just a bit surprised to see you."

"I should have warned you. I should have called. But I sort of did this on the spur of the moment."

"And if you hadn't done this on the spur of the moment, you might have changed your mind, right?" he asked with the arch of his brows, which were as dark brown as his hair.

Jase had always been a little too perceptive. "Right."

He moved a few steps closer to her. "How long can you stay?"

"I haven't decided on that yet. I took a leave of absence, but I won't overstay my welcome. I've always wanted to see Santa Fe and a lot of the Southwest."

"How did you get here? I mean, from the airport?"

"I rented a car. I wanted to be able to go where I wanted, when I wanted."

A slow smile curved Jase's lips...his very sensual lips. "In other words, you don't want me to plan your stay for you."

"Oh, I didn't mean—"

He laughed. "It's okay, Allison. And it's good to see some color in your cheeks again."

She only seemed to blush around him. It had always been like that, and he always noticed. In fact, the way he was looking at her now...

Virgil noisily stood up at his desk. "Aren't you going to introduce us, Jase?"

Jase flushed slightly himself, then introduced Allison to Clara Bush and Virgil Harrihan. After Allison shook hands with them, Jase didn't give any explanations about why she was there. He just said, "Give me two minutes to see if I have any important messages, and we'll go to my place."

After Jase disappeared down the hall and into an office, she could feel both Clara and Virgil's eyes on her. Sending them both what she hoped was a friendly smile, she went to the bench again to wait. But Jase was back before she could even sit down.

Opening the door, he motioned her to go ahead of him. Once they were standing on the steps, he said,

"I'll pull up in front of the parking lot. You can follow me, okay?"

She nodded.

Jase's head was still spinning as he drove about three-quarters of a mile, made two turns and stopped in front of his small ranch house, motioning Allison to park in the driveway. His pickup truck was in the garage and she could pull in beside it later. He still couldn't believe she was actually here.

He'd left Richmond five years ago because he couldn't handle watching her with his best friend. Allison was like a melody that had hummed in his heart ever since he'd met her in high school. But his trailer park background and her middle-class one were more than a railroad track apart. Her world was refined and comfortable. His was sparse and elemental.

Quickly climbing out of his SUV, he crossed to the driveway and waited until she opened her door. "Is your luggage in the trunk?"

She nodded.

"Go ahead and pop it."

After she did, he automatically went around to the back of the car and lifted out a suitcase and garment bag. He'd seen a travel bag in the front seat of the rental. He tried to see his house through her eyes. It was a chocolate-brown stucco with a flat roof. The crushed-rock yard was dotted with two junipers, prickly pear cacti and clumps of chamiso. Its greenish-yellow flowers were blooming now.

They walked up the path to the small concrete porch. He set down her suitcase to fish the keys out of his pocket, and she came up behind him.

"You're right. The sky *is* very blue out here."

For a moment he stilled and took a look at it. He'd

forgotten he'd said that. Everything here was a whole lot different than in Virginia—redder, browner, a different shade of green. But he forgot about the colors of the landscape as his gaze landed on Allison again. Her beauty always socked him in the gut. She looked so damn pretty today with a gold barrette in her hair at her temple, her cheeks slightly pink from the heat. Giving himself a mental shake, he opened the door and motioned her inside.

Before she stepped over the threshold, she gave him an uncertain smile.

If *she* was uncertain, he was doubly so. When he joined her inside, he wondered what the hell he had been thinking, telling her she could stay here! Looking around the place, he saw it as she did. The lodgepole pine furniture had been made by a local craftsman. The blue-and-tan Southwest-patterned cushions weren't particularly soft. He'd never bothered with drapes, just blinds. As he looked into the kitchen with its eat-in area, he knew these quarters were going to be tight for the two of them. She was used to mahogany and lace and plush carpet.

"I love the wood floors, Jase. They're beautiful."

The oak floor was one of the reasons he'd bought the house. "I suppose I should put a rug here or there and get some curtains. But I'm not home very much. C'mon, I'll show you to your room."

There were two bedrooms, and he took her to the second one. As he laid her suitcase on the bed and hung her garment bag in the closet, he glanced at her again. She was running her hand over the pine dresser, her delicate fingers almost caressing the wood.

Desire bit at Jase until he tore his gaze from her.

"I don't cook much," he said gruffly. "So I guess it's best if we go out for supper."

"I can cook if you'd like," she suggested softly. Her wide green eyes were so clear, so innocent.

"Absolutely not. You're my guest."

"I don't want to be a guest, Jase. I don't want you to think you have to feed me or pamper me or do anything for me. I can take care of myself. I *would* like to cook for you. That's the least I can do for you for giving me a place to stay."

The inside of the house was hot, and sweat was already beading on his brow. "I just hope you'll be comfortable here. The bedrooms have a western exposure with no shade, and they get pretty hot. I'll switch on the swamp cooler and see if it helps."

But he knew it wouldn't be the air-conditioning she was used to. A swamp cooler basically added humidity to hot dry air. And the ductwork for the cooler on this house was poorly positioned. The living room was the coolest room in the house, and that wasn't saying much when the temperature soared over one hundred degrees as it had today.

"I'd like to take a shower and change," Allison said, still gazing at him.

The thought of her in his bathroom, in his shower, made his house more ovenlike than it had been a few moments before. "Sure. I'll be around the back of the house checking the cooler. It was rattling last night. When you're ready, we'll go get something to eat. You can try your hand at cooking another time."

Before she could look up at him again with those big green eyes, he left the spare bedroom, wondering what the hell he'd gotten himself into.

Ten minutes later, Jase was returning his screwdriver to his toolbox when he heard the bathroom window crank open farther. He'd been trying to keep his mind on anything but Allison. He could too easily imagine her hair wet, her skin water slick.

"Jase?" her soft voice inquired from the bathroom window. "Are you there?"

"I'm here. Is something wrong?"

"I got into the shower in a hurry and didn't realize there weren't any towels."

He swore. After his shower this morning, he'd gathered them up and stuck them in the washing machine. Hopefully he still had one left in his closet.

Going over to the window, he gave himself high marks for nobility when he didn't try to look in. "I'll be right there." He smelled flowers as he walked away and suspected it was either Allison's soap or shampoo. With her in his house less than a half hour, he felt wrung out and ready for a stiff drink.

His linen closet was a few feet from the bathroom and mostly empty, but he found a utilitarian white bath towel and plucked it from the closet. Then he rapped softly on the bathroom door.

When Allison opened it, she was wearing a lavender and pink satin bathrobe belted at her waist. But she must have been sopping wet when she put it on, because it was clinging to her at places like a second skin. Her hair was dripping wet, and he realized he liked seeing her not looking quite so perfect. She hadn't opened the door wide, and she tried to stand behind it as he handed her the towel.

"Thanks," she said, pushing her wet hair over her forehead. "It was silly of me not to look before I got into the shower." Her green eyes met his, and he couldn't look away.

Moments ticked by as he was all too aware of her slender body under that robe. His own was responding to everything he could see and everything he couldn't—the scent of flowers, the sparkling clarity in her eyes that now weren't shadowed as they had been at his niece's christening. Maybe her trip here was doing her some good already. He had to remember she had been his best friend's wife. He had to remind himself of his past with women and the poor role model he'd had in his father, who'd cheated on his wife constantly and had finally run off with another woman altogether.

Tearing his gaze from hers, Jase said gruffly, "I'll get changed while you finish up. I turned on the cooler. Just leave the window in there cracked. Maybe we'll get a crosscurrent going."

As Jase turned away, she called after him. "Jase, thanks for inviting me here. I already feel as if—" She stopped.

He could only imagine how difficult this past year had been for her. She didn't have to explain. "A change of scene can work wonders."

After a momentary pause, she asked, "How should I dress tonight?"

"Anything goes at the Cantina, so wear whatever you want."

After another small smile, she closed the bathroom door again. Jase breathed a huge sigh of relief.

Allison sat beside Jase in his truck, which was a lot more comfortable than many cars she'd ridden in. But the seat was a plush bench seat, and she seemed much too close to him. She couldn't help thinking the feelings she was having were inappropriate. When he'd looked at her in her half-wet bathrobe, had she imagined that fire in his eyes? If it really *was* there, did she want it to be?

Jase had always been too much for her—too wild, too sensual, too savvy. She'd known his reputation in high school as the local bad boy, and she'd stayed away from him. Her upbringing had led her to fall in love with Dave Rhodes, a boy with a background similar to hers. Yet if Dave couldn't be faithful to her, a man like Jase probably wouldn't even try. She didn't think she could ever trust a man again, let alone trust herself to hold on to one. Dave's betrayal had shaken the very core of who she thought she was.

She'd taken off her wedding ring after she'd found the letters, so she *shouldn't* feel guilty every time she looked at Jase and felt the tingles in her body that had started at the christening. From the moment she'd entered the Richmond church, she'd been aware of his tall figure next to his sister in the pew. Arriving on his doorstep like this was totally out of character for her. But maybe she needed to do lots of things that were out of character to shake off the haze of grief, anger and doubt that had almost suffocated her for the past year.

The cantina was called exactly that—the Cantina. It was an adobe structure with a red-tiled roof. When Jase ushered Allison inside, the temperature was cool and comfortable. She'd worn a red-and-yellow-flowered sundress with a yellow bolero jacket. For the first time in a year, she'd wanted to feel pretty. Jase was wearing a tan collarless knit shirt and jeans that looked almost new. She'd never been so mindful of his muscled arms or powerful thighs and long legs as she was tonight.

When they stepped deeper into the tiled foyer, to her right Allison could see a smoke-filled bar lined with stools. The dining room straight ahead was decorated with piñatas and colorful tapestries on the walls. Black wrought-iron tables spilled out onto a patio, and a popular ballad flowed from a jukebox in the corner.

"We seat ourselves," Jase said. "Do you want to sit inside or out on the patio?"

"I like it in here." The atmosphere was colorful, the smells delicious and she actually felt hungry. If they sat outside and dusk fell, it would seem too intimate.

As Jase led the way to an empty table, he seemed to know everybody. She supposed being sheriff in a small town was almost like being everyone's guardian angel.

When they reached an empty table for two by the wall, Jase pulled out a chair for her. He pushed her in, and his arm brushed hers. She glanced up over her shoulder. Their gazes held for a few moments, and they both stilled. Allison was sure Jase could hear her heart pounding, but then he moved away and lowered himself into the chair across from her.

Taking the menus from between the salt and pepper shakers, he handed her one. "Do you like spicy food?"

"I've never eaten very much of it."

"Then you should probably go easy. The *pollo ranchero* is excellent. Sort of like a chicken fajita."

She examined the menu and the names of dishes she had no idea how to pronounce, let alone interpret.

Jase took a quick look at his menu and then closed it again.

"What are *you* having?" she asked.

"The tamales. Everyone says they're the best in the state."

"What do you recommend to drink?" she asked, looking over the list.

"*Horchata.*"

"What is it?"

"Do you have to know before you drink it?" he asked with a smile. "I promise it's not lethal."

"Or mind altering?" she asked with raised brows.

"Not a drop of liquor in it."

Smiling back at him, she said, "Okay, I'm game."

Silence stretched between them until he finally broke it. "Josefina and Ernesto go by the philosophy that once you come through those cantina doors, you should relax. So nothing happens in a hurry here."

She gave a little shrug. "When I got on that plane, I left schedules and responsibilities behind. This is perfect."

Crossing his arms on the table in front of him, Jase looked deep into her eyes. "Why *did* you get on that plane?"

"Because I needed to get away for a while," she answered quietly.

"You could have escaped to a thousand and one vacation spots. Why here?"

Her hesitation lasted a few moments until she managed to sort her thoughts. "I needed to get away from my parents and lots of friends hovering over me. But I didn't want to go somewhere where I didn't know anyone. Coming here seemed like the right thing to do." Jase's hands on the table were distracting. They were large and so very capable. If he ever touched her...

She fidgeted with the knife at her place setting.

Just then, the waitress came over to take their order. She was wearing a white peasant blouse and black slacks and looked to be in her thirties. "Hi, Jase," she said with a smile.

"Hi, Rita." He introduced Rita De Luca to Allison and explained, "Rita's married to one of my deputies."

"It's good to meet you," Allison said.

Rita's smile was friendly. "I hear you're visiting Jase for a while."

"Word gets around fast," Jase grumbled.

"You know Virgil. He can't keep anything to himself."

"You're married to Virgil?" Allison asked.

Rita laughed heartily. "Good Lord, no! Virgil's not married. Probably never will be. There's not a woman in Red Bluff who could put up with him. No, I'm married to Chuck. You'll meet him, too, if you're here long enough. So what would you like?"

After Rita had taken their orders, a slow ballad started on the jukebox. Two couples seated nearby strolled to the postage-stamp-sized dance floor.

Rita nodded their way. "Dinner will be a long time coming." She laid her hand on Jase's shoulder. "Take advantage of the slow one while you can. The group who just came in will make sure it doesn't slow down again the rest of the night."

A group of young adults looking as if they were out for a night of fun were pushing two tables together.

As Rita moved toward the kitchen, Jase asked Allison, "Would you like to dance?" He looked doubtful that she would.

Did he really want to? Or did he feel obligated because of Rita's suggestion? Suddenly it didn't matter, and she very much wanted the experience of dancing in the arms of Jase McGraw. She nodded.

After studying her intently, he stood. They walked to the dance floor together and for a moment, neither of them seemed to know what to do. The last time she'd danced with Jase had been at her wedding. But it had only been for a few minutes and she'd been so in love with Dave, so sure of the kind of future they were going to have and their happily-ever-after, that she hadn't been much aware of anything but him.

But everything had changed.

When Jase slipped his arm around her and she laid her hand on his shoulder, all other thoughts fled her mind.

The room wasn't hot, but she was getting hotter. When she dared to look up at Jase's face, his jaw was set and tense, his expression was unfathomable.

"This is a nice place," she said, trying to make conversation.

"Yes, it is."

"Do you come here often?"

His brown eyes seemed to grow browner. "It's the nicest watering hole in town. So I stop in."

His body was tense. She could feel his muscles under her hand as he held himself away from her. As if he didn't want to dance close. As if this was a duty dance he had to get through. He was much more distant than he'd been earlier. "Jase, we can just go back to the table. We don't have to dance."

"You don't want to dance?"

"It's not that I don't want to, it's just it seems as if *you* don't."

He blew out a long breath and looked chagrined. Finally his chiseled jaw jutted out a bit. "Look, Allison, I don't know if I should say this or not, but I'm going to. You were my best friend's wife. But you're a beautiful woman. It's hard for a man to dance with a woman and...and not get revved up. Not that it means anything," he was quick to add. "I know you came here for a vacation and nothing else, and I'm going to see you get one." Then he stopped dancing altogether and looked down at her intently. "I guess what I'm trying to say is that you're safe with me."

Now she realized why he was holding himself away from her. If they danced close— He'd said she was beautiful. Was he just being kind? Would he respond to *any* woman in his arms? Jase's reputation told her that was a possibility. And at this time she had so many doubts about her ability to attract a man and keep him interested.

It was better to act as if they were two friends who were going to be housemates for a little while. Jase had always been the type of man who protected and defended those around him. Over the years her trepidation in being around him had come from the feelings he stirred in her, never from anything he'd said or done. "I know I'm safe with you, Jase. I've always felt that." She meant it. She wouldn't have come here otherwise.

He seemed to relax a bit then and even brought her a little closer.

Jase smelled like man and forest. He must have shaved and dabbed on cologne when he'd changed. It felt so good to be held in his arms. She missed being held. She missed being touched. But when she thought of all the times she'd made love with her husband, she couldn't help but wonder what he'd been thinking. She couldn't help but wonder if he'd wished he'd been with his partner, Tanya, instead of with her. What had been real about their marriage and what hadn't been? What had been lies and what had been the truth?

Over the past year, she'd had so many doubts that a man could ever really want *her*.

Yet the look in Jase's eyes—

More couples joined them on the dance floor and his embrace tightened. He was guiding their movements with a brush of his thighs, with a slight pressure of his hand, and sometimes when they moved... He *was* aroused.

Allison had never felt like this dancing with her husband, and she experienced a mixture of guilt and excitement, as well as a yearning that seemed as foreign as the dishes on the restaurant's menu. When she looked up at Jase, his jaw wasn't quite as tense, but his eyes were shuttered as if he'd gone somewhere he didn't want anyone to follow.

"What are you thinking about?" she asked, hoping conversation would settle her down, would make everything seem more normal.

"Nothing that matters."

Jase had always been like that—closed with personal information, closed with his feelings. "It must matter if you're thinking about it."

He leaned away and gave her a wry smile. "Did they teach you that kind of logic in nursing school?"

"Nope. I came up with that all on my own."

His smile grew more genuine. "I was thinking about how far we are from Richmond. How far I am from the way I grew up."

Allison had never visited the trailer where Jase had lived as a boy. Whenever she'd seen him with Dave, it had been around Dave's home or at school. She'd heard from Dave about the trailer park, though. After her husband and Jase had gone through the academy and joined the police force, they'd gotten an apartment together. In the meantime, Jase's sister had gotten a scholarship to X-ray technician's school and eventually graduated, married and found a position at the Richmond hospital where Allison was a nurse. That's when Mrs. McGraw had sold the trailer and moved in with Patty and her husband. Jase had moved to New Mexico five years ago.

But moving on didn't mean forgetting, and she supposed Jase had a lot to remember. "Tell me about growing up," she prompted him.

He shook his head. "You don't want to know."

"I wouldn't have asked if I didn't want to know."

Lines around his mouth deepened as he frowned and appeared to be debating with himself. Finally he said, "It wasn't pretty, Allison. Patty and I didn't always know where our next meal was coming from, let alone our next pair of shoes."

"Your mom was a housekeeper, right?"

"That's a civilized way of putting it. She was a cleaning lady. The well-to-do folks don't offer many benefits and they think manual labor shouldn't command as high a wage as sitting at a desk shuffling papers."

"So it was just you and Patty and your mom?" That was about as delicately as she could ask about his father.

"Yep. Dad left the day after my tenth birthday." After a long moment, he added, "And I think that's about all the digging I want to do into my past tonight.''

It was a gentle rebuff, but a rebuff nonetheless and as they danced now, she didn't enjoy it quite as much. It was more awkward, and she was almost relieved when the song ended.

When they returned to the table, she saw their drinks had arrived. The *horchata* came in a huge glass with lots of ice and looked kind of milky. After they were seated, she asked, ''Are you going to tell me what's in this?''

''Try it first.''

She did. It tasted like almond and was very refreshing. ''It's good.''

''It's rice water and almond and sugar. Almost as good as beer on a hot day.''

Allison's knee accidentally brushed against Jase's as she shifted in her chair. He moved and so did she, but the feel of denim on her bare leg lingered. While she searched for a comfortable topic again, an exotic woman with a smile and long, dark brown hair that flowed almost to her waist came over to the table. She was much curvier than Allison, and her jeans and T-shirt emphasized every womanly dip and mound.

''You didn't tell me you were coming here tonight,'' the woman said in a teasing tone that was much too familiar for Allison's peace of mind.

''I didn't *know* I was coming here tonight,'' Jase answered with a grin that was totally relaxed. ''Maria Youngbear, meet a friend of mine from Richmond, Allison Rhodes.''

Maria extended her hand and Allison shook it.

''You're Dave Rhodes's wife?''

Allison nodded, wondering why this woman knew about her.

Maria exchanged a look with Jase. "Jase has spoken of his friendship with your husband. I'm sorry about your loss."

If Jase knew Maria well, they'd probably discussed everything about his background. Maria probably knew more about it than Allison did.

"Maria's a doctor at our local clinic," Jase explained. To Maria he added, "Allison's a nurse."

"You should stop in and see the clinic sometime if you're interested," Maria said brightly.

The invitation seemed genuine. "Maybe I will. It could be interesting to compare notes. I sometimes volunteer in the clinic in downtown Richmond. Would you like to join us for supper?" Allison asked, knowing it was the only polite thing to do.

"I'd like that, but I'm meeting a friend out on the patio. She's already here." Maria laid her hand on Jase's arm. "Don't work too hard."

"Take your own advice," Jase said with a knowing look.

Cocking her head, making her luxuriant hair ripple across her shoulder, Maria said to Allison, "Come visit anytime. I'll be expecting you." Then she walked away from their table toward the patio.

"How long have you known her?" Allison asked, trying to sound nonchalant, as if she was just making conversation.

Jase's gaze followed Maria, then swerved back to Allison. "Since she started at the clinic about a year ago."

"I guess your paths cross a lot in a small town like

this with you being the sheriff and Maria being a doctor.''

"You could say that.''

As before, Jase was closemouthed about his life. So Allison asked what she wanted to know. "Are you and Maria seeing each other?''

Chapter Two

Jase's brown eyes seemed to sear right through her. "Maria is married."

In spite of that, Allison sensed something between him and the beautiful doctor, and Maria wasn't wearing a wedding ring.

Allison knew Jase could be hard. He had a side to him that Dave had described as steel-like when he was determined or threatened. It probably stood him in good stead as a sheriff. Now she saw it in the unrelenting set of his jaw and the lack of warmth in his eyes.

When she didn't say anything but waited for a further explanation, he added curtly, "It's a long story and not mine to tell."

Obviously he wasn't going to say anything more, but an urge she didn't understand made her press anyway. "So you're friends?"

"Yes."

Door shut. Subject closed. Picking up his glass,

Jase drank a few swallows of his *horchata*. She followed the movement of his glass to his lips, the way he swallowed, and noticed his tan had gotten even deeper since his move to Red Bluff.

Their food arrived then and conversation didn't flow as easily as before. They talked about sights in the area Allison might want to see, and nothing else that was personal. Yet everything seemed personal suddenly, and Allison couldn't shake the feeling something had changed between them, shifting the type of friendship they'd always had.

In the cool restaurant, cups of dark, hot coffee seemed like a good idea after the spicy food. Music continued to play but Jase didn't ask Allison to dance again. She noticed customers now and then eyeing her with Jase, and she supposed it was a natural thing for people in a small town to keep track of a sheriff's private life.

"Do you feel as if you live in a fishbowl?" she asked him, as a woman taking a second glance at them passed by.

"Now and then. But it goes with the territory. When I'm on the job everyone has a right to know what I'm doing. If I want to keep my off time private, I go into Albuquerque or hike in the desert. It's easy to get away here—lots of wide-open space where no one cares what I'm doing or where I'm going. I can find isolation in fifteen minutes or less."

There had always been an aloneness about Jase. "Do you like being isolated?"

"There are lots of times I'd rather keep my own company."

This man might have been Dave's best friend, and he might have spent a lot of time at Dave's house because he preferred it to being at his own, but he was definitely a loner. "I don't want to get in your way while I'm here. If I do, just say the word and I'll go to a motel."

He frowned. "I didn't mean—"

"Oh, I know you didn't. But you're a man who's used to doing things his own way in his own time, and I don't want to disrupt your life." She thought again of Maria and what might be going on between the two of them. On the other hand, since Maria was married, she couldn't imagine Jase not respecting that. She wished that she knew the whole story.

"My life isn't easy to disrupt, Allison. I think it's more likely that you'll want to return to Richmond out of sheer boredom."

Bored? When every time she gazed into Jase's deep brown eyes, she felt the earth shake a little? Not likely.

The waitress brought their bill, and Allison opened her purse. But Jase shook his head. "My treat."

"You're not going to pay my way while I'm here."

He tilted his head. "I wouldn't think of it. Just consider this your 'welcome to Red Bluff' dinner that I would have cooked if I had the talent."

"Will you let me cook for you while I'm staying with you? I haven't much felt like it since—" She stopped. "There doesn't seem to be much point in cooking for one," she finished.

"If cooking for me means that you'll eat like you did tonight, then you go right ahead."

She'd been unaware of it, but she *had* eaten tonight, hadn't she? She'd practically finished everything on her plate. Since Dave had died she'd lost nearly ten pounds and it seemed Jase had noticed. But this trip was already helping her feel healthier and more alive.

Fifteen minutes later, Allison and Jase stepped into his house. The heat from the day had gathered and lingered and apparently wasn't going anywhere even with the cooler running. Although the temperature had dipped to the seventies outside, when a breeze blew, it was still a warm one. Jase went through the house opening all the windows, then returned to the kitchen.

The police scanner on the counter buzzed and he turned it up, listening to the calls for a few minutes. "It's a quiet night. Sometimes heat waves breed more accidents and emergencies." He took a quick glance at her. "What are your plans for tomorrow?"

"Sleeping late," she said with a smile.

His lips turned up in amusement. "I guess that *is* a luxury. I'll be up and out of here before six. I'll try not to wake you. I'm going to turn in. Feel free to watch TV."

"I brought along a couple of novels I haven't had time to read. I think I'll just settle in bed with one of those."

He nodded. "All right. Do you want to use the bathroom first?"

"No, you go ahead. I'll finish unpacking."

The house was filled with midnight darkness and quiet as Jase turned over in bed for at least the twentieth time, wiped beads of sweat from his brow, shook out his pillow and rearranged it under his head. He never had trouble sleeping. But tonight with the heat and with Allison only a wall away...

As he'd exchanged his clothes for sleeping shorts,

he'd heard her in her room. He'd heard her running water in the bathroom. He'd heard the creak of her bed, the click of her light. Was she asleep yet or could she hear him tossing and turning?

He was a man who knew his needs and had denied them as often as he'd satisfied them. Never before had he been around a woman who made him feel as if his self-control was on the edge of going up into flames. When they'd danced tonight, his complete arousal had unsettled him. Even now, just thinking about her—

He swore out loud and wondered if Allison had heard him through the thin wall.

Maybe if he got out of his room, forgot about the fact that she was actually a few feet away, he'd relax and then maybe be able to get some sleep.

When he stepped into the hall, he saw Allison's door was slightly open. She'd probably tried to get a crosscurrent going. The idea that she was sleeping in the bed just a few feet from the partially opened door...

The heat in his body, as well as his decency, urged him down the hall and into the living room. It was cooler there than in the bedrooms. One of these days he should have the ductwork redone. Striding toward the glass doors in the dining area, he opened them and stepped onto the patio outside.

Allison's soft, sweet voice came to him from a chair on the right. "Need a glass of milk?" she asked.

A three-quarter moon hung from a sky glittering with a thousand stars. In the pale light, Jase could see her easily. She seemed to glow under the light of the moon. Her blond hair was loose and slightly mussed, soft around her face, lying caressingly against her shoulders. As she stood, her bathrobe came open. She quickly belted it again, but not before he'd gotten a glimpse of her breasts pressing against satin. She seemed to shimmer as she stood there in the night's pale light. More sweat beaded on his brow. .

"I need more than a glass of milk," he murmured huskily.

It was too dark to see her blush, but he could imagine it as she gazed at his chest and the hair that arrowed straight down under the band of the sleeping shorts.

She attempted to slip by him. "I'd better go back in."

And he should let her go back in. But he couldn't. Before she could open the glass door again, he caught her arm. "Why did you ask me about Maria tonight?" He'd gotten the feeling her questions were more than idle curiosity, and he found himself hoping that was so.

"I...uh..." She licked her lips and his body responded to the glimpse of her tongue gliding over the pink skin.

"Does my personal life interest you?" he pressed, his voice going deep with the thought of it.

"You're single and—" She stopped again, then continued in a rush, "And free. She's beautiful and the two of you seem to have a connection."

"You didn't answer my question." He was still holding her arm and they were standing so very close. He could smell the sweetness and womanliness of her and his desire raged, hardly held back by the dam of nobility he'd erected where she was concerned.

"I was just curious," she murmured, her voice almost a whisper.

"Why?"

She looked like a deer caught in the glare of head-lights. If he pushed too hard, she might go back to Richmond. Or, if he pushed too hard, something might happen they'd both regret.

Before he kissed her in one of the thousand ways dancing through his head, he released her and stepped back. "Never mind. It doesn't matter. Try to get some sleep." In other words, *Go into the house before I do something that you'll regret or hate or feel guilty about later.*

Apparently she got the message. She murmured, "Good night, Jase," and stepped into the house and closed the sliding glass door.

He blew out a huge breath. He and Maria *were* friends. He'd met her and her husband as a couple. When Tony Youngbear had left four months ago because he'd wanted to follow a career path his wife didn't, Maria had been furious with him and felt deserted. She'd gone through a really tough stretch. Jase had been there to listen, and they'd become close. But it had never developed into anything more and never would. Maria was still in love with her husband.

But he wasn't going to parade Maria's heartache in front of anyone, not even Allison.

Still in love with her husband.

Allison was still in love with Dave Rhodes. When would she be able to stop grieving and really start living again?

Jase sank down into the patio chair. When she *was* ready to start living again, she needed a man who could offer her fidelity and a picket fence. His background and history told him he never could. How many times had he heard the maxim, "The apple doesn't fall far from the tree," let alone the phrase,

"He's just like his father"? Well, he wouldn't be just like his father, because he wouldn't hurt a woman by marrying her!

By tomorrow he'd wrap up his desire for Allison Rhodes and bury it so deep inside him it wouldn't surface again.

If Allison thought she'd sleep late Friday morning, she'd been mistaken. After her encounter with Jase on the patio in the middle of the night and the electricity that had made every nerve in her body tremble, she hadn't gotten to sleep for a long time. She'd blamed it on the heat, a strange bed, different surroundings. But in the truth of the morning light, she'd known it had nothing to do with any of those. It had to do with Jase and whatever was humming between them.

When had it started? At the christening? Throughout the years of friendship, when she'd hardly ever met Jase's eyes because they were too intense, because he was so very different from the boys and the men she'd known?

He'd always disconcerted her, and she'd dealt with that by never talking to him too long or getting to know him too well, or even standing too close.

So why had she made this trip?

To explore the unknown. It was as simple as that. But she didn't know how ready she was to explore it if Jase was a part of it.

After she dressed, she made herself a piece of toast and sat out on the patio in the shade for a long time. But she'd never been one to be inactive for very long and her thoughts were in a jumble she couldn't seem to untangle. So she decided to explore Red Bluff. Her atlas had numbered its inhabitants at around six thousand, but it was an old atlas.

Yesterday, after she'd deplaned, she'd found the address for the Red Bluff sheriff's office in the phone book. She'd headed straight there, not paying much attention to anything she'd passed. Today she wanted to find out why Jase had made his life here and liked it so much.

On the kitchen table this morning, Jase had left an extra key to the house and a second remote control for the garage door. His note had said simply, "So you can come and go as you please. Jase." Since she wanted to cook him supper tonight, one of her stops would be at a grocery store.

For the rest of the morning, she drove up and down the streets of Red Bluff, marveling at the difference between the landscape here and in Virginia. The high desert was indeed different from East Coast farming country. There were rocks and cacti and brush instead of green lawn. She still wasn't used to the reddish brown earth or the brightness of the sun. It seemed to touch everything with a dry heat, so different from the summer humidity in Virginia. She passed adobes and large estates. Jase had told her many of the residents lived here and commuted into Albuquerque, about forty-five minutes away. They apparently liked being outside of the hustle and bustle.

Cruising past a shopping center as she drove into the center of town, she made a note of it. When she drove by the sheriff's office, she wondered where Jase was and what he was doing.

A quarter mile down the road, she saw the sign that read, Red Bluff Clinic. Underneath in smaller letters was the name Dr. Maria Youngbear, M.D. Without hesitating, Allison turned into the paved lot and parked at the side of the one-story building. After she locked her car, she went around to the front and walked inside. Hispanic and Native American cultures mixed in the reception area with the bright-colored paintings and wall hangings. The waiting room was empty, and Allison saw the sign by the glass window at the receptionist's office. Doctor's Hours Today, 1 p.m. to 7 p.m. Allison glanced at her watch and saw that it was a little after noon.

The receptionist, a young woman in her twenties with light brown hair, looked up at Allison and opened the window. "Can I help you?"

"I'm visiting Red Bluff and I met Dr. Youngbear yesterday. She told me to stop in if I wanted to look around."

"She arrived a short while ago. Let me see if she's busy." The receptionist picked up the phone and pressed a button, telling Maria she had a visitor.

A few minutes later, Maria opened the door into the waiting room and saw Allison. "Hi, there! You picked a good time to visit. Come on back." The pretty doctor was dressed in jeans with a brightly patterned cotton blouse and sounded sincerely pleased to see her.

"I don't want to interrupt if you're busy."

"I was just going over some patient notes. I have a bit of time before the place starts jumping. Come on. I'll show you around." As Allison walked with the doctor down the hall, Maria asked her, "How long are you staying in Red Bluff?"

"I'm not sure yet. I don't want to get in Jase's way."

"Jase doesn't let anyone get in his way. What made you decide to take the trip out here?"

"I saw Jase at his niece's christening and he...invited me."

At that, Maria looked surprised. "I see. He never mentioned it."

The way Maria said that, it sounded as if she and Jase talked a lot about everything. Allison was curious about her story, but she didn't feel she could ask personal questions when they really didn't know each other. As Maria showed her around, Allison did ask other questions though. How long had the clinic been here? Who funded it? Was Maria the only doctor in town?

Maria explained the clinic had been established under a private endowment by a man whose family had lived in the area for four generations. Some patients came all the way from Albuquerque because they knew if they couldn't pay, they wouldn't be turned away. It had been in operation for a year now.

"We're understaffed, of course," Maria explained. "There's a retired doctor who helps me out, Dr. Grover, but he likes to keep his hours limited. I have an L.P.N. but I'd give anything to have a registered nurse on the staff."

When the tour was over, Maria smiled. "I'm glad you stopped in." She opened the door that went back into the waiting room, but now the reception area was full of patients. "Uh-oh. Full house today. I'd better get started."

Allison thanked Maria and waved goodbye, thinking about what it would be like to work at a clinic such as this full-time. It would be challenging working so far from other medical facilities.

After a stop at the supermarket where she purchased everything she thought Jase would like for a real home-cooked meal, Allison drove back to his house and carried the groceries inside. She'd planned to roast a chicken, stuff it with filling and make mashed potatoes. But as soon as she entered the house, it was so hot she thought about changing her mind. Still, she'd bought the food, and she wanted to thank Jase for his hospitality.

She stowed the perishables in the refrigerator, then changed from her jeans and knit blouse to her briefest shorts and a tank top. Having some time before she started dinner, she took a magazine out on the patio. A voice called to her from across the yard.

"Hello over there."

Leaving her magazine on the glass coffee table, Allison walked to where a petite gray-haired woman was standing by the split-rail fence. "Hi."

"It's unusual to see someone around Sheriff McGraw's house. You a relative?"

Allison suspected that the woman was watching over Jase's property for him. "No, I'm a friend visiting from Richmond. Allison Rhodes." She extended her hand.

The woman took it and gave it a firm shake. "I'm Gloria Torres, Jase's neighbor. I watch his house for him when he's not around. Do you know that man doesn't even lock his doors? Says he doesn't have anything worth stealing. Personally, I think it's kind of a dare. If anyone ever does take anything, he'll have the fun of chasing them down."

"Locking doors is a habit I wouldn't know how to break," Allison mused, thinking about her husband, thinking about the night he'd been caught in the middle of a gang fight and had gotten killed because of it. Bigger cities had their conveniences, but they had their downfalls, too.

"So you say you're a friend of the sheriff's. Have you known him long?"

Allison knew the woman was on a fishing expedition, but she didn't think Jase would mind if she filled her in a little. "I knew Jase in high school. He and my husband were best friends."

The woman's eyebrows raised.

Before a rumor got started, Allison continued, "I'm a widow now."

"It's nice to see Jase has some longtime friends. He's a loner, that one is. Has a reputation with women, too, from what I hear. But he doesn't bring them home. The only one I've ever seen here is Maria Youngbear."

Not particularly happy to hear that and eager to find out more, Allison said, "I met her last evening. I just came from the clinic. She showed me around."

"Hmm. When her husband worked there with her, we didn't have to wait so long."

"Her husband is in the area now?" Allison asked ingenuously.

"Goodness, no! He's over in Africa somewhere. Wanted her to go along but she wouldn't. So they split up. But they're not divorced yet that I know of. I'd have heard about it at the beauty parlor if they were."

Allison had to smile, even though the sun was beating down on her and she could feel perspiration between her shoulder blades. "Well, it was good to have met you."

"Same here. If you need anything while you're

here, you call me. Jase has my number on his refrigerator. I made him put it there.''

This woman would talk all day if Allison let her. She'd cared for patients like this who were simply lonely. ''It will be good to know someone's nearby.''

''If you want to come over and sit for a spell...''

She couldn't refuse Gloria altogether. ''Maybe another time. I need to get dinner started.''

''It's good someone's cooking for the sheriff. He stops at that fast-food place too much.''

It took Allison a few more minutes to finally end the conversation, but with a wave and a promise that they'd talk again, she extricated herself and went inside, thinking about everything Gloria had said, from Jase's fast-food meals to Maria's separation from her husband.

As Allison had driven around town this morning, she'd tuned into a local radio station. Apparently this hot spell was unusually severe. The temperature could hit 105 today. The house felt like an oven as she determinedly prepared roast chicken and stuffing, then peeled potatoes. Perspiration beaded at her temples, and she began feeling very tired. She'd found raspberries at the grocery store and she figured while the oven was already on, she might as well take advantage of it. Her mother had taught her how to make raspberry custard when she was a teenager, so she did that now, proud of the meal she was preparing.

When Jase came in the door around five, all she had left to do was to mash the potatoes and steam the vegetables.

As he entered the kitchen, he swiped his hat off and ran his hand through his hair. ''It's as hot as blazes in here.''

"We can take our plates outside to eat."

His gaze passed over her, and she realized she must look a mess with her damp hair and her tank top sticking to her. But instead of disapproval, there was a glint of gold in those brown eyes, and she was suddenly speechless.

When he approached her, she stood very still, then finally found her voice. "Why don't you change while I finish this."

His hand reached out, and she knew he was going to touch her. Smoothing back from her temple a few wisping hairs that were damp, he said, "Your face is flushed."

She gave a little shrug. "Like you said, it's hot."

"You didn't have to go to all this trouble." His husky voice was very gentle.

"It wasn't trouble. I enjoyed doing it. Go on and get changed, then we'll eat."

When he looked as if he wanted to touch more than her hair and his gaze dropped to her lips, she wondered what his kiss would feel like, taste like. But then he lowered his hand and stepped back. "I'll only be a few minutes."

As she set the food buffet-style on the kitchen table, fatigue from the afternoon caught up to her. She was removing dishes of custard from the refrigerator when he returned to the kitchen. But as she went to straighten, she teetered and Jase saw it. He was by her side in a moment, holding her shoulders to steady her.

"What's wrong?" he asked.

She was tempted to tell him nothing, but then knew she couldn't lie. "I just felt a little dizzy."

Taking the dishes from her, he set them on the

table. Keeping his arm around her waist, he guided her toward the door. "You're going to sit on the patio. You're not used to this altitude. Have you been drinking much water?"

"Not a lot," she responded, still feeling unsteady.

"You've got to drink plenty of water while you're here, especially in this heat. It keeps your body hydrated. I should have warned you. I didn't expect you to be doing hard labor in the kitchen."

"It wasn't—" she protested.

"Sit," he commanded as he brought her to a chair.

"Jase, I'm perfectly capable of getting my own plate."

"Sit," he commanded again.

Wrinkling her nose at him, she murmured, "Just because you're bigger and stronger and a sheriff, you think you can tell people what to do."

"You bet."

Knowing it was useless to argue with him, she lowered herself into the chair.

"You're not going to move until you drink at least two glasses of water and eat supper. Got it?"

With all the energy drained out of her, she simply nodded. The first thing Jase did was bring her a tumbler full of water. She drank it down and then he brought her another glass and a plate filled with food.

They ate in silence for a while until she finally ventured, "How was your day?"

"Nothing unusual."

"I visited Maria's clinic."

He leaned back in his chair. "What did you think?"

"It's a nice setup, but she's understaffed. Working there would be challenging."

After examining her again closely, he asked, "How are you feeling?"

"I'm fine, Jase. Really. Like you said, I just didn't realize I wasn't used to the altitude. I'll remember to drink more."

"And take it easy."

"We'll see."

His eyes narrowed. "At least stay out of the heat. In fact, I think we should sleep in the living room tonight. I usually do that when the temperature goes this high."

She wasn't sure exactly what he was suggesting. "You sleep on the sofa?"

"You can have the sofa. I can make up a bedroll on the floor."

"I don't want you to have to sleep on the floor in your own house!"

"I'm used to camping and bedrolls on the ground. I grew up sleeping above Patty in a bunk with no springs, just a thin piece of foam. So you don't have to worry about me bedding on the floor. Do you think you can sleep on the sofa?"

Sleeping on the sofa wasn't the problem. Sleeping in the same room as Jase *was*. "I could start out in my bedroom."

"No, you can't, Allison. It's ten degrees warmer in there thanks to the western exposure and poor ducting for the cooler. In fact, I think we should go into Albuquerque and buy a box fan to really get some air going."

"No one in Red Bluff has any?"

"They're sold out. Do you feel up to a drive?"

"Sure. I told you I'm fine. But I'd like to shower and change first." Standing, she was about to stoop down to the table for her dish and glass when Jase stood before her.

"You're really feeling okay?"

"Yes. It was stupid of me not to remember I was in a higher altitude. I'll take a bottle of water along on the drive."

"Not stupid," he said gently. "Just a bit forgetful. Thanks for dinner. It was great. I only get meals like that when I go home."

The trace of a smile on his lips made her want to smooth her fingers over them…and more. "You're welcome," she murmured.

Their toes were almost touching. The line of Jase's beard was becoming more visible. This near to him…

"Allison." Her name was a question and a request and a protest. She knew what he wanted and she wanted it, too. So she didn't move when he bent his head. She didn't tear her eyes from his. She didn't breathe.

Jase's arms went around her as his mouth came down on hers. The swirl of sensations that overtook her made her world sway again. She reached up around his neck to hold on tight. He groaned as her breasts touched his chest. His tightened hold, along with the invasion of his tongue, made her feel desired and womanly and totally lost in a sensuality she'd never known.

But then he tore his mouth from hers and raised his head. The expression on his face caused her to pull her arms from around his neck and drop them heavily to her sides.

"I never should have done that," he said raspily as he backed away.

"It's okay, Jase."

"No, it's *not* okay. You came here to recover from the last year, not complicate it. Go on and change. I'll clean up the kitchen while you're getting ready."

Did his backing away have to do with her, or did it have to do with him? Maybe the kiss hadn't been that exceptional to him. Maybe the excitement she'd felt was all one-sided.

Hadn't Dave proved by his affair that she was sorely lacking in the siren department? That she couldn't give a man what he wanted? Still filled with doubts, embarrassed by the way she'd thrown her arms around Jase's neck, she fought back tears that quickly pricked in her eyes and turned away from him toward the door.

"I won't be long," she murmured as she pushed back the screen and stepped inside, not wanting Jase to see how devastated she was by his lack of desire for her, or by the consuming feelings that had thrilled her in their kiss.

Chapter Three

On the drive to Albuquerque, Jase was silent. Allison didn't try to start a conversation, thinking they both needed some time to forget about the kiss on the patio. The problem was, she wasn't forgetting. Her insides were still trembling and she kept remembering his taste, his embrace.

They drove across land that looked as wild and primitive as the passion she'd felt in Jase. He fit out here, with the heat and the wind and the starkness. It all seemed so strange to her.

When they reached the city limits, he started acting like a tour guide. She listened, but her attention was on his voice, his profile, the movement of his hand on the steering wheel. Finally he pulled into a shopping center, then came around and opened her door for her. They didn't touch and were careful not to brush against each other as they walked inside an appliance store.

Choosing a fan was easy for Jase. He seemed to

know exactly what he wanted. As he took out his credit card, she asked, "Are you sure the bedrooms won't cool down tonight?"

His expression took on that hard, determined look. "Believe me, the living room will be cooler. We'll both get a better night's sleep in there."

That kiss had erased the easy camaraderie between them. It had changed everything. She felt as if she didn't know what to say or how to act.

It only took Jase a few minutes to load the fan, and then they were on their return trip to Red Bluff. During the drive back, he slipped a cassette into the tape player on the dash. It was fifties music and, in spite of the tension between them, she had to smile. Jase belonged back in the fifties with the likes of James Dean. All he needed was the black leather jacket.

When they turned into his driveway, he switched off the cassette and climbed out. Then he glanced at her briefly. "Just prop the screen door open for me."

She met him at the tailgate and, seeing lights in the house next door, remembered her conversation with Gloria. "I met your neighbor today."

"Gloria?"

"Yes. She's quite a talker."

He opened the tailgate. "That's one way of putting it. If you talk to her longer than two minutes, she'll know everything from your birthday to your favorite flavor of ice cream."

Allison laughed. "She seems nice enough."

"Oh, she is. A mother hen. She insists on watching over me even when I don't want her to."

"She thinks you eat too much fast food."

That brought a smile to his lips. "She's probably

right about that. What other tidbits did she offer you?''

He was pulling the fan from the bed of the truck when Allison said, "She told me about Maria."

Instead of picking up the carton, he looked over at her. "And exactly what did she tell you?"

"That her husband wanted to practice medicine in Africa and she didn't, and that they're separated."

He frowned. "I guess if you have to sum it up, that's the best way to do it. Gloria's a nice lady, but she's a gossip, too, so be careful what you tell her." He seemed to think for a few moments, then he turned to look at her again. "Did Gloria say anything else worth noting?"

Allison could deny that she had, but there was something else and she wouldn't mind seeing Jase's reaction to it. His face was shadowed, but she could see his rugged contours in the light of an almost-full moon. "She said you date a lot of women, but Maria's the only one you bring home."

"I don't *date* Maria," he said firmly with an undertone of anger.

"She's separated and her husband is miles away," Allison prompted, knowing she should let the subject go but unable to.

"I've had my share of women, Allison, and none of them have been married. But if you want to believe a nosy neighbor, you go right ahead."

She wanted to believe *him.* She wanted to believe there was nothing between him and Maria, yet she knew there was something. Maybe he was denying it or maybe he couldn't see it. Then again, she didn't know the whole story. It was obvious she wasn't going to get it from Jase, at least not now, not tonight.

When he hefted the box into his arms, closing their discussion, Allison went ahead and opened the door.

Although the temperature outside had cooled at least thirty degrees, the inside of the house was still hot.

"Why don't you go out and sit on the patio? It's cooler. I'm going to get this set up, then take a shower."

She didn't care about being cooler; she'd rather stay in here with him. She couldn't understand this newfound curiosity to observe the way he moved, the way he looked, the expressions flitting across his face when he let them.

But after the way he'd reacted to their kiss, he might not want her close by. "All right," she said, as her chin went up a little and her shoulders squared. "I'll be on the patio." Then she went to the kitchen, took a pitcher of water from the refrigerator and poured herself a glass.

Jase swore under his breath as he tore open the fan's carton. He didn't want to give Allison the impression he didn't want her around. But he might have. He'd handled tonight poorly. But she definitely threw him off balance. And that kiss...

He'd kissed women before. He'd kissed lots of women before. But he'd never felt so shaken as in those few moments when overwhelming passion had coursed through him like fresh new blood loaded with fire. Even if she'd wanted the kiss, even if she'd been curious about the chemistry between the two of them, she was still grieving. She was still in love with Dave. He'd be an absolute fool to take advantage of that. He'd be an absolute fool to think he could settle down with one woman now. Or ever.

Settle down?

That wasn't even in the realm of possibility. Allison lived in Richmond. He lived here. She was as fresh and green as the Virginia countryside. He was as dusty and sharp as the cliffs and bluffs dotting the New Mexico landscape. They were water and oil, spring and winter, and he'd better remember that before they both took a tumble off a cliff that they wouldn't recover from.

Half an hour later, Jase went outside where Allison was sitting on a lounge chair, looking up at the night sky. She was bathed in the glow of stars and moonlight and seemed almost ethereal. She was a dream that was as far out of reach as the North Star. "We're all set," he said gruffly. "I have some extra sheets in the closet. If you want to grab a pillow from your bed, we can turn in whenever you're ready."

She looked over at him then, but only for a moment. Her gaze slipped from his and she stood. "You're the one who has to get up early. I'll only be a few minutes." When she disappeared inside, he felt frustrated with this new awkwardness between them. The kiss had done that. In the morning maybe they'd both forget about it.

The trouble was they had to get to morning.

A short time later Allison came into the living room in her nightgown and robe with her pillow under her arm. Jase swallowed hard. Her robe was tightly belted at the waist, but that didn't hinder his imagination one little bit. In fact, all he could think about was untying that belt, slipping the robe from her shoulders and kissing the bare skin underneath.

He'd spread a sheet over the sofa and now she sat

on it, waiting for him to use the bathroom before she took off her robe.

When he reentered the living room in his sleeping shorts, she was lying on the sofa on her side with the sheet pulled up to her shoulder. Working together, the fan and the swamp cooler had drawn out some of the day's heat. But he imagined that the sheet protected her modesty more than it protected her from drafts.

"Don't worry about waking me in the morning. I'm usually an early riser," she murmured.

He'd made up a bedroll on the floor about three feet away from the sofa. The living room simply wasn't that big, and he'd had to push the coffee table underneath the window. Lowering himself to the bedroll, he stretched out and faced her, propped on one elbow. "What are your plans tomorrow?" It was Saturday, but he was working.

"I don't have specific plans. I might just putter around here. I want to explore Albuquerque, but I need a street map to do that."

"I can take you to Albuquerque on Sunday, and we can go sightseeing if you'd like."

"Are you sure you want to do that?"

It was obvious she didn't want to impose on him, and he wondered how she thought that she could. "I wouldn't have offered if I didn't want to. Besides, believe it or not, there are parts of Albuquerque I haven't even seen yet."

"I'd like to go then. I'd like to take in as much as I can while I'm here. Once you show me around, I'll be more comfortable doing it on my own."

He didn't like the idea of her doing it on her own. He couldn't remember her being this independent when she was married to Dave. It was as if she had something to prove, as if she didn't want to depend on a man. He couldn't help staring at her hair falling softly over her cheek, her sheet draped above her breasts.

For her part, she was avoiding his gaze. Now she reached for the table lamp beside the sofa and switched it off.

As they lay in the darkness, he was arousingly aware of Allison within an arm's reach.

He heard her sheet rustle and then she said, "Jase, if you usually go out Saturday nights, I don't want to…disrupt your plans in any way. I can always find something to do on my own tomorrow night."

His reputation as a swinging bachelor was more fiction than fact these days. "I'll be working a long shift tomorrow," he said tersely. "At least till seven. So I don't have any plans."

"Oh," she responded softly. "Would you like me to fix a late supper?"

"That's up to you." He didn't want to get too used to her being here. He didn't want to get too used to coming home to a meal. He didn't want to get too used to anything about Allison Rhodes, because she'd be going back to Virginia and her life there.

Settling on his back, with his hands under his head, Jase knew it was going to be a very long night.

When Jase drove Allison to Albuquerque on Sunday, her heart felt almost light. She'd had a quiet day yesterday while he was gone, reading, sitting on the patio with a cool drink, napping in the afternoon because she hadn't gotten much sleep the night before with Jase lying only a few feet away. She'd made a stir-fry for supper so as not to heat up the kitchen as she had the day before. With it they'd had salads and the rest of the raspberry custard. Jase had poured them each a glass of sangria, and they'd eaten on the patio. They'd kept the conversation on anything and everything that wasn't personal, and when they'd turned in for the night, there'd been electricity charging the air, but not the awkwardness of the night before.

This morning Allison had awakened before Jase and had gotten a shower and dressed before they could get in each other's way. Because whenever their arms brushed or their eyes met, she felt as if the whole world trembled. She didn't know what Jase felt.

Even now, he looked almost relaxed, but there was a guardedness about him...something that hadn't been there before they'd kissed.

He drove her to Old Town Albuquerque and parked. As they walked down the street, she liked its ambience immediately. There were shops and restaurants and galleries, along with adobe homes. All of it was very old world, steeped in history. She'd never seen anything like it. In each shop she found new treasures to appreciate. When she saw a ceramic pot in the colors of earth and sunset, she knew she wanted to buy it for Jase's kitchen table.

While he was looking at artifacts in a glass case, she purchased the pot and then crossed to him. "This is for you."

His look was one of almost pure astonishment. "You didn't have to buy me anything."

She smiled. "Of course I didn't, but I wanted to. Just consider it a thank-you present."

He took the pot from the bag and examined it carefully, turning it around, studying its shape and the colors. "It's a beautiful gift, Allison. When I look at it, I'll remember your visit." Putting it back in the bag, he tucked it under his arm. "Where would you like to go next?"

She was glad he'd accepted her gift in the spirit in which she intended it. She never knew what Jase's reaction would be. "I saw a used bookstore about two stores up. I'd love to explore there for a while."

After a nod, he opened the door for her so she could precede him outside. He'd left his Stetson at home today, but in his light blue polo shirt, jeans and boots, he still looked like a cowboy.

Once in the bookstore, Jase struck up a conversation with the proprietor, a Hispanic man who looked to be in his forties. Allison wandered here and there, picking up first a volume of this and then a volume of that.

She was paging through a leather-bound book of Robert Frost's poetry when Jase came up beside her. "Find anything interesting?"

"I'd buy half the store if I could. I love old books. Dad used to read me *Treasure Island* and *Robinson Crusoe* while Mom read me poetry. What do you like?"

"I'm not much of a reader," he said gruffly. "We never had books around the house. My father read comic strips and if he caught me with a book, he'd tell me my time was better spent learning how to do something useful, like fixing a car engine or the drip in the faucet." Jase's tone was more sad than bitter.

"I can't imagine not having books around," she mused. "They opened up worlds to me. They kept me from being lonely when no one was around. They made me want to learn more about so many things.

And there's something about poetry…'' She shook her head. ''It's like watching a sunset with so many changing colors, only the poet uses words to create the beauty instead.''

He was studying her carefully. ''I learned about the world in my own way. A much different way than you did.''

At that moment, she realized how very different they really were. Jase had grown up on the streets, learning reality early. She'd grown up protected from the harshness of life, and from its thrills. Was this attraction she felt for Jase intriguing because they were so different?

She slipped the volume of Frost back on the shelf. ''I'm ready whenever you are.''

The differences between them seemed to be a barrier as they toured Old Town Albuquerque, then had supper at an outdoor café. Most of the shops had closed by the time they finished their meal, but as they wandered along the street, Allison stopped in front of a store window. It was a jewelry store with everything from liquid silver necklaces to conch-shell belts on display.

What caught her attention most were barrettes fashioned of semiprecious stones—turquoise and agate, lapis and onyx. ''Oh, I wish they were still open. I'd love to have one of those.''

''We'll have to come back before you leave.'' As they walked to the Jeep, Jase suggested, ''If you aren't tired, there's someplace I'd like to take you.''

''Where?'' she asked.

''A spot west of the city.''

Something in his voice told her it was someplace

special, someplace he wanted to share with her. "I'm not tired. Let's go."

As Jase drove, the shadows grew longer and Allison saw red peaks rising before her. Soon they were well out of the city. The landscape zipped by and she tried to take it all in, knowing she'd want to remember it when she went back home. Right now home was far away, and she liked the fact she wasn't colliding with memories around every corner.

Jase veered off the beaten track and bumped over a gravel road, stopping not far from the cliffs. She was wearing espadrilles and, as he opened her door and held out his hand to help her disembark from the truck, he looked down at them. "You're going to have to be careful."

His grip was strong and supportive as she jumped to the ground. "I will be."

He showed her to a path, then they climbed side by side until it became steeper, rising in huge steps that were naturally part of the landscape. Jase went before her, holding out his hand, helping her reach the next one until they stood at the top of a flat area as big as a small room. He pointed to the west. The sky was a palette of brilliant orange, light pink, a deep rose and purple swathed with blue. In the midst of it, the sun was a fire-filled ball sinking lower each second, making the colors shimmer and glow against red peaks.

She'd never seen anything like it. "Oh, Jase, it's beautiful."

They were standing shoulder to shoulder facing west. Now he looked down at her. "I didn't want you to leave without seeing this at least once."

"I'll never forget it," she murmured, and felt tears in her eyes.

Gently taking her chin in his palm, he nudged her gaze up to his. "What's wrong?"

"You've given me a beautiful memory."

"I'd imagine you have lots of beautiful memories."

She tried to blink the tears away. "Not as many as you think," she whispered.

When she attempted to turn away from him, he caught her shoulder. "What do you mean?"

She hadn't told anyone about Dave's infidelity. She didn't want pity, or judgment that she didn't know how to deal with. Jase was the last person in the world she wanted to tell. The fact that her husband had had an affair made her look weak and foolish and altogether insecure.

"It's just..." she began, and then stopped.

Jase's thumb caressing her cheek prompted her to continue.

"It's just that when you lose someone, memories you thought were happy ones can become sad ones."

"I'm sorry you lost him, Allison."

She felt like a hypocrite. On one hand she did miss Dave, but on the other hand she was so angry and hurt at his betrayal that she wished she didn't. And the thoughts filling her head right now shouldn't even be there. She was wondering what she would have to do to make a man like Jase be faithful to her. What about herself would she have to change? Apparently she wasn't sexy enough or Dave never would have...

"What's running through your mind?" Jase asked huskily.

She couldn't tell him. She couldn't tell him his best

friend hadn't been an honorable man. She couldn't tell him her thoughts seemed inappropriate a year after her husband's death. She couldn't tell Jase she wanted him to kiss her again.

The wind blew her hair across her cheek.

She thought he bent his head. She thought he was going to kiss her again. But then his jaw hardened and he retreated a step. "We'd better get back to the truck before it gets dark. Come on. I don't want you to trip and fall."

Allison drew in a breath of air that was cooler than it had been an hour before, knowing she should be glad Jase had backed off.

Because she had no idea what to do with a man like him.

Around noon on Monday, Allison was preparing herself a salad for lunch when she became aware of the flurry of noises coming from the scanner. It was turned down low, but she could tell from the back-and-forth responses that something had happened somewhere. She was about to turn it up when the phone rang in the kitchen.

Picking up the cordless phone, she said, "Sheriff McGraw's residence."

"Allison, it's Jase."

She'd pretended to be asleep this morning when he'd left. Sleeping in the same room with him was so darned...intimate, and the push-pull tension that strung taut whenever they were together seemed worse in the dark. She'd heard him tossing and turning during the night, and she'd tried not to do the same. Now she heard something in his voice that told her he wasn't calling to tell her he'd be late for supper.

"There was a bus accident outside of town. It was a bad one. The bus rolled and I don't know how many passengers were injured. Maria's taking charge and her clinic is the clearing point for anyone not seriously injured. But Dr. Grover is out of town and, if you're willing, she could really use your help."

Allison knew she couldn't practice in New Mexico without being licensed here, but she couldn't *not* help in this type of emergency. Besides, most states had a Good Samaritan law...

Her training took over. "Do you need me on the scene or at the clinic?"

"On the scene until we get the most seriously injured patients taken care of. The Medevac chopper is on its way. I swear, if the driver who made the bus swerve off the road has any alcohol in his blood—" Jase swore.

"Where are you?" Allison asked, already hurrying into the bedroom with the phone to fetch her keys and purse.

Jase gave her his location, then said, "Thanks, Allison. I really appreciate this."

Didn't he realize no thanks were necessary?

After she hung up, she exchanged her sandals for her sneakers, tied her hair back in a ponytail, and practically ran to the garage.

When Allison arrived at the site of the accident, everything was chaos. There were patients on stretchers, ambulances, onlookers milling about, and Jase and his deputies doing what they could, where they could. The sun blazed down on all of them from high in the sky. When Allison saw Jase helping a couple into his Jeep, she went over to him.

"Scrapes and cuts," he said. "I'm taking them to the clinic. The Medevac will be here any minute for Maria's patient. You should probably go over there first."

Allison saw Maria by the side of the road in the shade of a police cruiser and hurried to her. She was inserting a bore needle in a woman's chest. Allison guessed that a fractured rib had pierced a lung. If so, it was serious and the woman could die. She nodded to Maria and knelt down by her side. "Is there anything I can do?"

The young woman on the ground had huge, dark brown eyes and straight black hair. She looked to be about twenty-one and terribly frightened. "My baby. What's going…to happen…to my baby?" Her breath was labored.

Maria patted her arm. "He'll be fine, Cecelia. We'll take him to the clinic until we find out exactly how serious your injuries are."

"But who will…take care of him? I'm breast-feeding and…" Tears ran down her cheeks.

"Where's your husband?" Allison asked gently.

"He's in California, traveling on business. I was…visiting my aunt…taking the baby back home to wait for George…" She winced, and Allison could see that she was in pain and that her worry was making it worse.

Suddenly the young mother caught Allison's hand. "Promise me, you'll…take care of Pablo. I don't…know what I'd do…"

Allison squeezed Cecelia's hand. "I promise."

Hearing the sound of a chopper, Allison looked up and could see it coming their way.

Then everything happened fast. The paramedics got an IV line going and had Cecelia loaded into the helicopter in a matter of minutes.

As the chopper rose and headed to Albuquerque, Allison asked Maria, "How serious do you think her injuries are?"

"A rib fracture with a collapsed lung." Because there were still more patients she hadn't seen yet, Maria said, "Come on. You can help me triage the rest of the passengers. We're sending the more serious injuries by ambulance back to Albuquerque. Virgil, Chuck and Wyatt are helping to transport patients to the clinic."

For the next half hour, Allison made sure Cecelia's son was taken back to the clinic with Connie, the L.P.N. who promised to look after him, then she worked side by side with Maria, helping where she could. She lost sight of Jase until he came over to her with a straw hat in his hand and plopped it on her head. "If you don't want to get a sunstroke, you'd better wear this."

The heat was so dry out here compared to Virginia that she wasn't as conscious of it. "I'm fine, Jase, really."

"Don't argue with me, Allison. It's probably 110 in the sun today. You don't want to be one of the patients rather than their nurse. Listen to what I'm telling you." He handed her a bottle of water.

Looking around, she saw that she wasn't needed anywhere for the moment. Touching the brim of the hat, she asked, "Where did you get this?"

He pointed to an elderly lady sitting in his Jeep.

"She wanted you to have it. You can give it back to her when you get to the clinic."

"What about Maria?"

"Maria's used to this climate. You're not."

Allison took the bottle of water from him, uncapped it and took a few swallows. "Thanks for looking after me."

He mumbled, "Somebody's got to. I'm going to take these patients in. I'll see you in a little while."

After everyone who was more seriously hurt was transported to Albuquerque, Allison drove to the clinic, meeting Maria there. Then she worked side by side with her for another hour, helping in whatever way she could. She was aware of Jase coming and going, but had no time to speak to him again.

It was almost four o'clock when she heard the sound of a baby crying. The L.P.N. brought little Pablo, just waking from a nap, into the examining room where Maria and Allison had just finished with a patient.

As the crying became howling, Allison instinctively reached out to take him from the nurse's arms. When she put him to her shoulder and swayed back and forth with him, he quieted.

Jase had followed the L.P.N. in. "I guess I'll call social services and see if they have someplace for him until we hear about the mother."

"Do we have to do that?" Allison asked, remembering her promise to Cecelia.

"What's the alternative?" he asked her.

"I told Cecelia I'd see that he was taken care of. Can we take him back to your place?"

Chapter Four

Jase was looking at her as if she'd lost her mind. "You've got to be kidding."

"I'm serious, Jase. Someone's got to take care of Pablo. At least for tonight. And I promised Cecelia I'd keep him safe. I know it's an imposition, but—"

"I don't know a damn thing about taking care of a baby." He looked absolutely horrified at the thought.

Smiling at him, she explained, "Their needs are really quite simple. You keep them fed, and dry, and give them lots of love."

After listening to the exchange, Maria finally piped in, "If this is really a problem for you, Jase, I'll make some calls."

Pushing the brim of his Stetson higher with his forefinger, he gazed at Allison and the baby cuddled so comfortably on her shoulder. "You're sure you want to take this on?"

For some reason, taking care of Pablo seemed very

important to her. "Yes, I am. We'll have to get some supplies—diapers, formula, a crib or cradle."

The L.P.N. who'd brought the baby in smiled. "I have a crib I use when my grandchildren come over. You're welcome to it."

With a shrug of resignation, he decided, "I suppose we can do it for tonight. Make a list of what you need and I'll go get it."

Allison knew she'd put Jase on the spot and she'd have to make it up to him. Crossing to the doorway where he stood, she lowered her voice. "When you get bottles, try to get the ones that are most like a woman's breast. The nipple's kind of scrunchy and flat."

A dark flush stained his cheeks as if he was uncomfortable talking about this in public. "That's necessary?"

"Cecelia was breast-feeding. Since the baby's also been using a pacifier, I'm hoping a bottle won't be a problem. Those nipples will help."

"Right," he muttered.

She almost smiled at his chagrin but successfully kept the corners of her lips from twitching.

He looked around Allison to Maria. "How much longer will you need her here?"

"We're almost caught up. Maybe another hour."

He nodded. "All right. Make the list and I'll go round up everything. Then I'll take you back to the house. I'll have Chuck or Virgil drive your car home."

"Thanks, Jase," she said softly.

But he just shook his head. "You're doing a decent thing. I'll help you as much as I can."

An hour later, Jase was back at the clinic, ready to

take her home. When they arrived at the house, Allison noticed right away that the swamp cooler and fan were running, and there was a collection of baby paraphernalia everywhere. In the kitchen she saw a box of bottles and liners for them. Disposable diapers were stacked on the kitchen table. Jase had positioned the small crib in a corner of the living room, and she took Pablo to it now and laid him down.

"I have to get a bottle ready for you," she said quietly. "But I promise I won't be far away."

The little boy raised his arms and batted them at her as if he understood. She caught sight of Jase watching her from the doorway. "He won't bite, you know," she teased. "At least not much yet."

Jase just shook his head. "You're good with him. How do you know what he needs?"

"I don't exactly. But he's dry for now. He slept most of the afternoon and had some applesauce a little while ago. If you want to hold him, feel free."

Jase shook his head. "I think I'll pass."

While Allison opened a can of formula and prepared a bottle, Jase went to the phone and dialed a number. A few seconds later, she heard him say, "Fourth floor nurses' desk." After a pause, he identified himself. "This is Sheriff McGraw from Red Bluff. I'm checking on a patient that was taken in by Medevac. Her name is Cecelia Natchez. Can you tell me her condition?"

A few minutes later he thanked the person he'd spoken to and hung up the phone. "They inserted a chest tube for her collapsed lung. She's resting comfortably."

Allison crossed to the living room. "I want her to

know her baby's well taken care of so she doesn't worry about him."

Following her, he assured her, "I'll call again later and see if we can't get a message put through to her. I have to go back to the office to take care of paperwork about the accident. Will you be all right here?"

Allison glanced at Pablo. "We'll be fine."

There was a knock at the door, and Allison saw Gloria standing on the small front porch.

Jase went to the screen door and opened it. After Gloria came in, she went immediately over to Pablo's crib. "Oh, isn't he adorable? I heard there was an accident and you brought the baby home. Do you need some help?"

Jase looked partly exasperated and partly irritated, but Allison smiled kindly at Gloria, knowing the woman just needed to be involved in other people's lives. "Sure, you can help. I was just about to feed him."

Jase shook his head. "I'll be back in a couple of hours, but I don't know when. So don't worry about saving any supper for me."

Pablo had begun whimpering and now it was turning into a full-fledged cry.

Allison went to the baby and picked him up. "I'll make tuna salad or something, then you can have a sandwich when you get home."

But Gloria chimed in, "Or I can make us a nice frittata. That will be heartier for a man like the sheriff."

Jase just rolled his eyes. "I'll see you later."

As Allison watched him leave, she wished she could get a real sense concerning how Jase felt about children...whether he was uncomfortable about Pablo because he'd never been around babies or because he wasn't interested in ever having any. Maybe later she'd ask him.

The sun had long ago set by the time Jase parked in front of his house. He'd tied up all the loose ends he could at his office, making sure every *i* was dotted. Sure, he was always thorough, but tonight he hadn't wanted to come home. Seeing Allison with the baby caused a hurt way down deep inside that he didn't understand. She was so easy with the child, so perfectly motherly.

When he stepped over his threshold, he stopped and stared. Allison had pulled the cane-backed rocker from her bedroom into the living room. She was giving the baby a bottle while she rocked. The expression on her face as she looked down on the little child with so much tenderness did something to Jase's insides.

Hearing him, she raised her head and met his gaze. "Hi."

He saw right away that her time in the sun without a hat had made her cheeks and neck very pink. Her arms were pink, too. "You got burned," he said brusquely.

Her eyes widened. "Some. I haven't had time to think about it. I fixed you a plate and left it in the refrigerator if you want to warm it up. Gloria's frittata was good."

He took a few steps closer. "Did she talk your ear off?"

"Actually she was a big help. We bathed Pablo in the kitchen sink. Have you heard any more about Cecelia?"

"She's resting comfortably and I told the nurse to give her your message. You can probably call her tomorrow. They're still trying to get in touch with her husband. He's on a business trip in California."

With the bottle finished, Allison sat Pablo on her lap and rubbed his back. He burped then grinned at her and reached for her hair.

Jase mumbled, "I'm going to get supper."

It didn't take long for Jase to finish the plate that Allison had prepared for him. Drinking a few swallows from his can of soda, he carried it with him to the living room. Allison was still rocking the baby and humming softly. It looked as if Pablo was asleep.

"Don't you want to put him in his crib?"

"I love holding him. I wish—" She stopped.

Sure he heard a quiver in her voice, he asked, "What do you wish?"

"I wish I'd had a baby."

The pull toward Allison was so great, Jase knew he couldn't keep his distance. He lowered himself to the sofa and faced her. "Why didn't you and Dave have children?"

She didn't answer for a moment, and her eyes grew shiny. "I'd rather not talk about it."

This surprised him, and he decided not to let it go. "Can you have children?"

Standing with Pablo, she took him over to the crib and gently laid him down.

Jase came to stand beside her and clasped her elbow. "Allison, can you have children?"

"As far as I know, I can."

It wasn't like her to be evasive, so he pressed further. "Could Dave?"

"I don't think he had a problem."

Frustrated now, Jase asked, "Then why didn't you have kids?"

There was so much turmoil in her eyes for a moment, he couldn't believe it. Finally she said, "It just hadn't happened yet."

That wasn't turmoil he saw, he told himself sharply. It was grief. She'd obviously longed for a baby with her husband, but his death had cut short their future. Apparently she was still trying hard to accept that.

Heat from the day warmed the house. The fan helped to promote crosscurrents and bring some cooler air in from outside, but it was having a tough time and so was Jase. Allison's shimmering green eyes were like the finest emeralds. Her blond hair was loose, not caught by a barrette, and damp tendrils wisped along her cheeks. The pinkness of her skin reminded him how she'd cared for everyone who'd needed her help without thinking about herself. The urge to kiss her was mighty strong.

Suddenly she asked him, "Why haven't you ever married?"

She obviously didn't want to talk about what she'd lost. But marriage wasn't a subject *he* cared to explore. Yet she deserved an answer. "Do you want the truth?"

She nodded.

"I never thought I could settle down with one woman. I don't know if any man is capable of committing to one person for the rest of his life."

"I see." There was something in her voice that was almost resigned…disappointed.

What had she expected? She knew his reputation, and he'd always thought what he'd just told her was true. Yet when he looked at her, he almost believed being faithful to one woman was possible. Still he could never take the chance of hurting a woman the way his father had hurt his mother. He remembered her tears and her heartache before and after his father had left her.

Allison avoided his gaze and crossed the room to the hall, but then she stopped. "Do you have anything I can put on the sunburn?"

"Sure, in my bedroom. I'll get it."

She waited for him to pass by her and when he did, he saw her eyes were filled with pain. Was it from the discussion they'd had about babies...about Dave's death? He certainly didn't want to cause her more pain, yet part of him wished she could forget Dave and her marriage. Part of him wished she was really free. But free for what? An affair?

That's what he was used to. Maybe it had just been too long since he'd bedded a woman, but Allison seemed so tempting right now. Maybe it was just that they were sleeping in the same room. If only the damn weather would cool off.

He could do a rain dance, he supposed, then almost smiled at the ludicrous thought. He just needed some perspective. Allison had only been here a few days. He'd get used to her soon.

He found the cream in his top dresser drawer and when he turned to hand it to her, she was standing by his king-size bed. The thoughts that suddenly filled his head made him think he was the one who'd been out in the sun too long.

He thrust the jar at her. "Don't worry about returning it. I have another."

When she moved to leave his room, he called to her, "Allison?"

She turned.

"You really need to buy some sunscreen."

He thought he saw a flare of temper in her eyes and told himself he imagined it, because she responded in a soft voice, "I'll put it on the top of my shopping list."

Allison lay on the sofa—hot, yet covered by a sheet because of Jase's presence three feet away—staring up at the ceiling, getting angrier and angrier. What was the point of marriage vows if a man couldn't be faithful?

Was Jase right about men needing more than one woman? Was a good marriage a dream rather than a real possibility? Were men such physical creatures that satisfaction and pleasure were more important than love and belonging? Or was it simply that a woman wanted to create a home, a safe, comfortable place where love could flourish, and most men felt stifled by that and wanted risks and thrills and adventures to forestall boredom and aging?

Allison thought about her parents' marriage. The truth was, she didn't know much about it. She'd imagined they'd had their ups and downs. Over the years she'd heard them arguing or disagreeing, but she'd also seen them hugging and kissing. They seemed to enjoy being together. But she'd thought Dave enjoyed being with her, too! She'd thought they'd been happy.

Rebelliously she swished off the sheet. She was hot, and if Jase could lie there practically naked in sleeping shorts, she didn't have to protect her modesty with a cover. In fact, soon she was going to buy some nice cotton shorty pajamas and pack the satin nightgown back in her suitcase.

She was thinking about getting up to get a cold drink when Pablo began stirring in his crib. At first she just heard restless movements, but then he started crying and she quickly got to her feet, hoping to quiet him before Jase awakened.

Going over to the crib, she lifted him to her shoulder. He was wet, and she thought he might even be hungry again. His cries swelled, filling the room until Jase sat up and rubbed his hand over his face.

"I was hoping he'd sleep through the night." Allison jiggled Pablo and patted his back.

"He's in a strange place without his parents. I guess I'd wake up yelling, too."

She couldn't help but smile. Jase was being a good sport about this. Taking the baby into the kitchen, she laid him on the blanket she'd spread out on the table where she'd set the baby wipes and a stack of disposable diapers. In a matter of minutes she had him changed, but he was still crying.

"What can I do?" Jase asked from her elbow.

When she looked up, her breath caught. His hair was sexily rumpled, a beard shadow swathed his jaw, and his furry chest was almost brushing her shoulder. The band on his sleeping shorts rode below his navel, and she couldn't help but imagine...

"Allison?"

Dragging her gaze up to his, she thanked the Lord for her sunburn, because she knew her cheeks would be as red as rouge. "Uh, can you get a bottle from the refrigerator? I filled some. Just run it under the hot water for a few minutes."

Jase did as she requested while Pablo squirmed at her shoulder. She shifted him to her other arm. When Jase turned off the water, he faced her and froze. Her nightgown strap had fallen down over her shoulder and her breast was almost bare.

Turning her back to him, she repositioned the strap, then lifted Pablo away from her. "Just a minute, little man." Without looking into Jase's eyes, she took the bottle from him and went to the rocker.

Still squirming, Pablo finally settled down to drink. He was all sweaty, though, and Allison decided washing him with a cool cloth would probably help. He made quick work of the bottle, and she set it on the coffee table as she settled him on her knees.

This was her chance to see what Jase really thought about babies. Standing, she held him out to Jase. "Hold him for a few minutes, will you? I want to get a cool cloth and wash him off."

Startled, Jase nevertheless took the baby from her almost automatically. "But I don't know *how* to hold him."

So he said, she thought. But she watched as he nestled Pablo in the crook of his arm.

"You're doing just fine. I'll be right back."

Feeling some satisfaction that she'd thrown him off guard and rattled him a little, she took her good time in the kitchen. She found a washcloth in the drawer, rinsed it under the cold water, then wrung it out. When she came back into the living room, Jase was sitting on the sofa with Pablo on his knee. There was something about his large hands holding the baby steady, the intent, concerned expression on Jase's face as he looked down at the little boy, that made Allison's heart ache. Somehow she'd known he'd be good with children. Somehow she knew that Jase's strength of character would lead him to be a good father.

"These diapers have got to be hot," he muttered. The outside plastic stuck to Jase's knee as he went to pick up Pablo again.

"They're absorbent," she said pointedly.

"They're also expensive. How long does a kid wear them?"

She had to laugh. "That depends on whose book you read. But until they're two-and-a-half or three."

Jase whistled through his teeth. "That's a hell of a lot of diapers."

While Jase held Pablo, who was quiet now and cooing at him, Allison gently took the soft cloth over the baby's face and then his arms and hands. "Feel better?" she asked with a smile.

"I need someone to do that to me," Jase mumbled.

Her gaze collided with his. He'd meant it as a joke, but as they sat there staring at each other, she could imagine taking a wet cloth over his tanned skin, and her whole body trembled.

He broke eye contact first. "Think he's ready to go back to bed?"

"I hope so. You need your sleep."

Jase carried Pablo to the crib and laid him down. The baby stilled, made a few cooing sounds and seemed to settle.

When Jase turned away from the crib, he was so close to Allison that his chest hair almost brushed her arm. His gaze dropped to her breast, the one that he'd seen nearly bared, and he said in a deep husky voice, "I need more than sleep."

As his arms went around her, she didn't resist. His

lips came down on hers, and she closed her eyes, telling herself this was a mistake, telling herself she should pull away. But she couldn't pull away from the seduction of his lips. She couldn't pull away from the invasion of his tongue. Rather, she tentatively touched him back, and he groaned. His hands slid under her hair, and she grasped his shoulders.

But at the feel of his taut muscles under her fingers, she realized what she was doing. She realized what *they* were doing. And she remembered what Jase had said. *I never thought I could settle down with one woman.*

How could she do this? How could she even think about doing this? Pushing away from him, she broke free and wrapped her arms around herself.

His breathing was as ragged as hers. "I can't say I'm sorry about that, Allison."

She couldn't say she was sorry, either. That was the problem. "Do you want me to leave?" she asked in a small voice.

"Do you *want* to leave?"

"No, but I can't..."

He rubbed his hand up and down the back of his neck. "I know you can't. I promise you it won't happen again unless you want it to."

She looked up at him then, wanting another kiss, wanting even more than a kiss. But *want* had nothing to do with this. Apparently wanting had ruined her marriage. Maybe Dave couldn't control his wants, but she could sure control hers. She didn't want an affair with Jase McGraw. She didn't want a vacation that she'd regret more than she wanted to remember.

"I'll go sleep in my bedroom," Jase said.

"But it's so hot."

"Not any hotter than it is in here right now. If you need anything, yell. If not, I'll see you before I leave for work."

And he strode down the hall.

Allison realized, whether he was out of sight or not, she wanted him to hold her in his arms.

She'd better get a grip on her emotions and her hormones or she'd have to fly back to Richmond before she was ready and make sense of her life there.

Jase was working late in his office the following evening, trying not to think about Allison at home with the baby, when Virgil stopped in the doorway. "I'm heading on home."

Jase looked up from the paperwork on his desk and nodded. "See you tomorrow," he said absently.

But Virgil didn't move on out. "I guess there's going to be a ban on fireworks for the Fourth this year."

"I got a memo to that effect. It's just too dry again. I put more patrols on for tomorrow night."

"They always find somebody who's too stupid to listen to reason," Virgil offered. After a pause, the deputy shifted on his feet again. "I heard that Chuck and Rita are throwing a party for Clara's birthday on Saturday. Are you going?"

"I suppose I'll stop in. Things have been a bit hectic and I haven't given it much thought."

"Yeah, I heard you have a kid at your place, along with...your friend."

Virgil usually wasn't subtle and Jase knew this had some kind of point, but wasn't sure where it was going. "Not much longer. The mother's doing well and the father's flying in from California. He was on a business trip and they just got hold of him.''

''Getting much sleep?'' Virgil asked.

''Enough,'' Jase answered noncommittally. He knew better than to go into detail.

Finally Virgil stepped deeper into Jase's office. ''I was just wondering…what kind of present do you think Clara might like? I mean, you've had a lot of experience with women and all.''

Irritated by the reference to a past he was trying to come to terms with, Jase tried to see what Virgil really wanted. Suddenly the barbed interchanges between Virgil and Clara became a little more clear and so was the reason why Virgil hung around the office when he didn't have to. His deputy was interested in his dispatcher. That almost made Jase smile.

''Women usually like candy and flowers,'' Jase recommended. ''But they also like you to notice what they like.'' The barrette that Allison had seen in the shop window in Albuquerque came to Jase's mind.

''You mean like those swingy earrings Clara sometimes wears?''

Jase thought about his dispatcher's penchant for dangling earrings. ''Yeah, something like that.''

With a loud interruption, Jase's intercom buzzed.

He picked up the receiver. Virgil would have left, but Jase motioned him to stay as he listened to what Chuck was saying. It was the kind of news he didn't like to hear.

He told Virgil, ''Chuck has already called for assistance at the Morton place out on Sandy Top Road. A gang of teenagers was shooting off firecrackers and some of them got hurt. He says a few are burned, but none look serious enough to call an ambulance. He wants to round them all up and take them to the clinic. I'll call Maria. Can you get out there and help?''

For a big man, Virgil could move fast. He tossed back over his shoulder, ''I'm on my way.''

Quickly dialing, Jase reached Maria at home and told her what had happened.

''I'll be at the clinic in five minutes,'' she said. ''Dr. Grover is out of town until next week and Connie's away for the holiday. I know Allison isn't licensed to practice in New Mexico, but it would help if she could come to the clinic and keep her eye on the boys until I can get to all of them.''

''She still has Pablo,'' Jase reminded her.

''Couldn't you watch him for a while?''

Jase thought about the baby and how Allison was taking care of him so easily. Then he remembered holding Pablo last night and he figured a man had to do what a man had to do. ''Yeah, I can. Give her a call. Tell her I'm on my way home now.''

When Jase walked into his house a few minutes later, Allison was dressed in jeans with her hair tied back. She was sitting at the kitchen table with the baby, feeding him applesauce. ''Maria called about the boys.''

Jase went over to her and held out his arms to the little boy. ''Come here, partner. It's you and me for a while.'' He could do whatever had to be done. He'd learned that at a young enough age to reinforce the fact that it was true.

But Allison was looking at him with concern. ''Maria said you're going to watch Pablo. Are you sure you're okay with that?''

''It won't be for that long,'' he said, taking the baby from her.

"But..."

"I promise I won't drop him," Jase snapped, wishing he could get control of everything rioting inside him every time he came within a foot of Allison.

She looked hurt at his abruptness. "I didn't think you would. I just wasn't sure you were comfortable caring for him. But if you think you can manage, open a new can of formula if he needs it, and if you think he's hungry, mix a little bit with his cereal. He likes it mushy, but not real wet."

"Got it," Jase said.

With a last, uncertain look at him, she kissed Pablo on the forehead, then stepped away. "You know where I'll be if you need me."

He didn't respond as she waited a moment and then hurried out the door.

He wouldn't need her. He couldn't need her, because he'd just end up hurting them both.

Chapter Five

Allison couldn't believe her eyes when she returned to Jase's house from the clinic around nine o'clock and saw him stretched out on the bedroll on his back with Pablo sitting on his stomach. The baby was waving his arms, grinning and cooing, and Jase was talking to him as if he'd been taking care of babies for years.

"Do you like that?" his deep, masculine voice asked. "Do you?" Then he tickled Pablo's bare belly and they both laughed.

"It looks as if the two of you are having a good time," Allison commented as she laid her purse on the kitchen table.

"We were just trying to occupy ourselves until you came home. I took him for a walk and then we sat out on the patio for a while counting the stars."

After transferring Pablo to the bedroll, Jase sat up. His red T-shirt was worn and soft looking. His denim shorts bared his long, tanned legs. He was wearing moccasins and his hair was mussed. With his beard shadow and smile, he took her breath away.

She couldn't let him see that and she managed, "So what number did you count to?"

His gaze stayed on hers. The whir of the fan in the silence seemed to emphasize all of the currents that rippled between them.

"We counted to two hundred," he said, his voice a bit raspy. "But then Pablo decided he wanted a snack. Oh, by the way, your mother called."

"My mother?"

"She seemed awfully surprised you'd given her my number. She thought she was calling a motel."

Allison's parents had been on vacation themselves. Before she'd flown out of Richmond, she'd written a note and left it on their kitchen table where they would find it when they came in. She'd just told them she had to get away for a while and not to worry and that she'd be in touch, hoping they wouldn't call her but would wait for her to call them. Obviously, she should have known better.

"What did you tell her?"

"I told her you'd call her when you got in."

Allison glanced at her watch. "I see. I guess I'd better call her then. But I really should change Pablo and get him ready for bed."

"I can do that. Go ahead and make your call."

Apparently Jase and Pablo had bonded, and taking care of the baby didn't seem awkward to Jase anymore.

He added, "I'll take Pablo into the living room. That will give you a little privacy."

She was probably going to wish she had a *lot* of privacy, rather than just a little.

As she picked up the phone, Jase asked her, "How did it go with the kids?"

"They were lucky. Virgil drove one of them to the emergency room in Albuquerque, but Maria took care of the rest. And Chuck gave them a lecture they're not going to forget anytime soon. Unfortunately, teenagers have this mind-set that they can do anything they want and nothing's going to happen to them."

Jase stood, letting Pablo play with a rattle on the bedroll. "I know they do. I was like that myself. I remember some of the pranks we pulled. But you don't want to hear about them. Go on and make your call." Then he crouched down and scooped Pablo into his arms. They were such strong arms. He was such a strong man. He was wrong thinking she didn't want to hear about his escapades as a teenager. She did. She wanted to know everything about him.

As she dialed her parents' number, she watched Jase and Pablo. He caught her looking and she glanced away, concentrating on the phone ringing in Virginia. On the second ring, her mother answered.

"Hi, Mom," she said simply.

"Allison. Thank goodness you called! I was so worried about you."

The truth was, Allison appreciated all her parents' concern, but it was getting to be more of a burden than a help. "I told you in the note, Mom, there was nothing to be concerned about. I needed a vacation myself. How was your trip to New England?"

"New England was beautiful as it always is. But that's neither here nor there. Why did you give me Jase McGraw's telephone number?"

Surreptitiously, Allison tried to see if Jase was listening, but she couldn't tell as he changed Pablo's diaper with a little bit of fumbling but more determination. She took a deep breath, bolstered herself for her mother's reaction, then answered, "I'm staying with Jase."

If she expected a sound of startled surprise, or admonition, she got neither. There was complete silence. Concerned they'd been cut off, Allison asked after a few moments, "Mom?"

Her mother's voice was quiet and sad. "I know Dave's death hurt you. I know you've been grieving terribly. But acting impulsively or recklessly isn't going to help anything."

Trying to stay calm, she explained, "The trip might have been impulsive, but it's not reckless. You've got to admit, Mom, I needed a change. When I saw Jase at his niece's christening, he told me I could stay with him if I wanted to get a taste of the Southwest. You should see the scenery. It's—"

"If you want to see scenery, you could stay in a hotel and take guided tours. You don't have to stay with a man who—"

This time Allison cut her mother off. "A man who was a respected member of the Richmond Police Force? A man who was my husband's best friend? A man who is now the sheriff of Red Bluff?"

"He had a reputation, honey. What will people think?"

"What people, Mom? I won't tell anybody in Richmond if you don't."

"I'm getting your father. Maybe he can talk some sense into you."

"Mom, you don't have to…" But there was silence again on the line. Then she heard her mother's muffled tones, and finally her father picked up the receiver.

"Hello, Dad," she said, knowing she was going to have to go through the whole thing all over again.

But he surprised her. "Hi, honey. How's the weather out there?"

She had to smile. When her dad didn't know what to say, he talked about the weather. "It's hot, and it's dry. But everything is so different that the world seems new again."

"How are you feeling?" he asked.

"I'm feeling good."

"Are you eating?"

"More than I have in a long time. I like the spicy food."

"And you're staying with Jase McGraw?"

"Yes, I am. He's been very kind. He took me on a tour of Albuquerque on Sunday, and right now, we're taking care of a baby."

"A baby?"

"It's a long story. The baby's mother was hospitalized after an accident, and we're just watching over him until he can be with her again. I like it here, Dad, and I feel…" She stopped, not wanting to say too much. "I feel as if I'm doing more than going through the motions."

He cleared his throat. "And McGraw's behaving himself?"

She wasn't sure how to answer that one. Maybe the question should be—was *she* behaving herself? "Most of the time he works long hours and I don't even see him. You know how seriously lawmen take their jobs."

After a pause, her dad asked, "When are you coming home?"

"I don't know yet. I took a leave and was planning on staying a few weeks. There's a lot to see."

"I imagine there is."

"Dad, please tell Mom there's nothing to worry about."

He chuckled. "Okay, I'll try to settle her down. But it would help if you'd call every few days so she knows you haven't been abducted permanently."

Allison laughed then. "All right. I'll do that."

A few moments later, she said goodbye and hung up, then turned to find Jase standing directly in front of her.

"So they gave you the third degree?"

"Dad seemed to understand. My mother, well, I think she puts too much stock in appearances. She always worries about what the neighbors will think. The truth is, most of the time, neighbors don't have an inkling of what's going on at all."

He studied her speculatively. "And that means?"

"That means no one really knows what someone's life is like unless they're living it."

His brow creased and his gaze became searching. "I'm kind of surprised you're staying here myself. You were always such a proper lady."

"And just what is a proper lady, Jase?"

His cheeks flushed slightly. "I meant it as a compliment."

"All right, then I'll take it as one. But what do you mean by a proper lady?"

She'd obviously put him on the spot, and he thought about it a good long while before he answered. "A proper lady always does the appropriate thing. She knows how to dress, she knows how to talk, and she knows when to use her salad fork.''

Allison laughed at that. But then she became very serious. ''I don't know if I'm a proper lady or not. But I do know I needed a friend more than I needed to worry about propriety. You've been that, Jase.''

''I haven't done anything.''

''Yes, you have. You opened your home to me. You've let me upset your life. You're even sleeping on the floor so I can be comfortable. But most of all, you're helping me to forget, and that's what I need right now.'' She needed to forget how her husband was killed, how she'd poured all she was into their marriage, how Dave had betrayed everything she'd thought they'd had. ''I can forget here with you, Jase. I'm somebody different here.''

The fan whirred; her heart pounded; Pablo made soft sounds in the living room as their gazes held.

''What happens when you go back?'' Jase finally asked.

When she went back, she'd relive Jase's kisses, and she'd remember every touch. ''I'm not sure,'' she murmured.

His hand slid along her cheek then, and he lifted her chin, rubbing his thumb over its delicate point. ''I want to be your friend, Allison. But I think it's damn hard for a man and woman to be friends when there's attraction between them.''

''It wasn't always there,'' she said, thinking out loud.

''Wasn't it?''

His eyes were as dark a brown as she'd ever seen them, and she didn't like what he was suggesting.

"You were Dave's best friend. I never even thought about—"

"So it suddenly sprang up between us when you arrived in Red Bluff?"

"Yes! No! Oh, I don't know, Jase." Had the attraction been there for years and she'd denied it...or run from it?

Jase shook his head. "That's what I thought. A proper lady doesn't entertain those kind of thoughts. A proper lady looks the other way, never acting on impulse. A proper lady falls for one man and doesn't look at anyone else for the rest of her life."

He sounded so bitter and resentful that she declared, "That's what fidelity and commitment are all about."

His expression became hard, and he dropped his hand. "Yeah, well, I'm no proper gentleman, and I don't know anything about fidelity and commitment. I know about taking, not giving. About using pleasure to get through a night, and then moving on the next morning. We're as different as Richmond and Red Bluff, Allison."

"What does that mean?" He seemed to be trying to scare her off, to give her plenty of reasons not to get too close.

"It means I slept in the bedroom last night because I'm not some nice guy who's sleeping on that bedroll every night with thoughts as pure as snow."

The desire flickering in his eyes was seductive and so tempting. "Maybe I don't want your thoughts to be as pure as snow."

Her soft words made him swear. "Maybe you don't know what you want, but I do. You're not the kind of woman who can have a one-night stand and not have regrets and guilt and maybe even shame afterward.''

Stepping around her, being careful his arm didn't brush hers, he reached for his keys where he kept them on the windowsill above the sink. ''I'm going out for a while. I'll try not to wake you when I come back in.''

He was already at the door when she called, ''Jase.''

But he shook his head. ''Let's drop it, Allison. If you want a friend, I'll be your friend. Anything else would get much too complicated for both of us.''

When he disappeared into the garage, she felt tears burn in her eyes. She wanted to be more than friends with Jase McGraw. She was falling in love with him.

At the Cantina, only two stools were empty at the bar. Jase slid onto the end one, not in any mood to talk. When the bartender said, ''Howdy, Sheriff. What will it be?'' Jase answered, ''A double whiskey.''

He hardly ever drank, maybe because he'd seen his dad loaded once too often. Maybe because from his job, he knew how alcohol affected the senses. But tonight he needed it. He needed the burning heat going down his throat and into his gut so he'd forget the other kind of heat. So he'd forget about Allison.

It was odd, but having that baby in his house made wanting her seem even more demanding. He didn't understand it. He didn't understand her. She said she'd loved her husband with all her heart. It was obvious she was still grieving. Maybe she was trying to forget too hard. Maybe she thought the chemistry between them would chase the grief away. But she was wrong.

He'd known Allison Rhodes for years. She had a conscience and values. Sure, he could give her a night of forgetfulness. But he didn't want her to hate herself in the morning, and he sure as hell didn't want her to hate him.

When a jeans-clad man in a dark brown Stetson slid onto the stool next to him, Jase thought about ignoring him, but then he saw who it was. Frank Nightwalker. Frank owned a ranch on the south edge of Red Bluff, and Jase had gone riding there a few times. Frank was as much a loner as Jase. Though Jase had had conversations with Frank over the past four years, he really didn't know him well. He knew the man had Cheyenne heritage, was proud of it, and that his ranch was his life. But that was about it.

The bartender set Jase's drink in front of him.

Frank noticed it and smiled. "You going to do some serious drinking tonight?"

Jase stared at the drink and deliberated a few moments. He didn't want one drink, he wanted about ten. Yet he wouldn't do that to himself or to Allison. The last thing he needed was for his control to slip even a little. So much for the burning distraction of alcohol.

"No, I'm not." Jase sighed. He said to the bartender, "Get me a root beer."

When the man's brows raised and he looked pointedly at the whiskey, Jase said, "I'll pay for that, too. Just get me the soda."

Frank pushed his hat farther back on his head. "Well, you don't own horses so you don't have an ornery one who's causing that crease in your brow. And it looks to me as if you're going to be a shoo-in for the next election for sheriff. So," he drawled, "my next best guess is that you've got a woman problem."

"I never had one that was a problem before," Jase muttered.

Frank laughed. "Uh-oh. It sounds more serious than something a drink's going to settle. Now me, I'm just thirsty." He said to the bartender, "Give me a Miller draft."

The two men were silent until the bartender set a mug before Frank.

Frank had a reputation for being friendly but keeping to himself most of the time. Jase always missed having a father he could turn to for advice, and Frank had always seemed like the paternal sort. "Were you ever married?" Jase asked, not quite sure how to get into the conversation he wanted to have.

The noise in the bar filled up the quiet until Frank said, "Once, a very long time ago. Why do you ask?"

Jase gave a nonchalant shrug. "Just wondered. I haven't been around many marriages that lasted. Statistics say only fifty percent do, and of that fifty percent, I wonder how many are really happy."

"I'm not the one to ask. Mine lasted five years, and during those five years—" Frank shook his head "—we had too much family interference to be happy. But it was my own stupidity thinking it would work. Me—an Indian, her—a one-time debutante with a father who had more control over her than he had money in the bank. And he had a hell of a lot of money in the bank." With a shake of his head, Frank sighed. "I tried to live in her life for a while and under her father's thumb. But I couldn't. There were too many differences between us."

There were so many differences between him and

Allison, Jase thought, he couldn't count them all. Frank's story was confirming his own conclusions. A man couldn't change his habits, or his beliefs, or who he was. If he tried, he was looking for trouble.

Frank took a few swallows of beer, then set his mug down with a thump. "The problem is, two people just don't mess up their own lives. I could have forgotten about my ex over the years, but I have a son and daughter back in Maryland I don't know. Their mother and grandfather wouldn't let me know them. And after I left, they wouldn't let me see them. I never had the kind of money I'd need to fight in court. As the years passed, it just got to be too late. My boy would be about your age about now I reckon. Thirty-three, thirty-four?"

"Thirty-four," Jase answered with a nod. "What's his name?"

"Mac. MacMillan Nightwalker. Unless they convinced him to change his name so there was no trace I'd ever been in his life."

The pain and regret and bitterness that Jase heard in Frank's voice warned him what happened when a man tried to cross too many lines, when a man tried to be something he wasn't.

"I don't talk about it much," Frank said. "It sure doesn't help. But that doesn't mean you can't talk about what's bothering you."

"What makes you think something's bothering me?"

"Because you ordered whiskey and you're drinking soda."

Jase gave the older man a wry smile. "I guess you don't believe I intended to use the soda as a chaser."

Frank chuckled. "Not likely. I imagine this all

might have something to do with that woman who's staying with you?''

Jase just shook his head. "Did somebody post it in a town bulletin?''

"You're the sheriff. People watch you."

Wearily Jase rubbed the back of his neck. "Allison's from that other world back east you spoke of. She's refined and sweet and entirely too vulnerable right now for me to let anything happen."

"Then you'd better send her back to where she came from before something does."

"I can't. When she got here she was as pale as a lily and wasn't eating. Now she's got an appetite and energy and the sparkle's back in her eyes. I've just got to keep her occupied, keep us both occupied. A friend's having a party Saturday night, and I guess I could take her sightseeing again," he said, thinking out loud.

"Bring her out to the ranch. Go riding. In fact, come over Sunday for supper. It's been a long time since I had some company."

"You're sure?''

"Absolutely. I even have a secret recipe for sauce for ribs. And I don't need much notice. I'll be making the ribs anyway so I have supper for the week."

Jase didn't think being alone with Allison for a whole day on Sunday would be good for either of them. Frank's invitation would help the situation immensely. "I'll ask her, then give you a call."

When Jase let himself into the house after midnight, it was dark, except for the small fluorescent light burning over the sink in the kitchen. He tried not to make any noise as he used the bathroom, then undressed in his hot bedroom. Too hot to get any sleep. He'd been awake most of last night. After convincing himself not only would he sleep better, but Allison might need help with the baby, he stretched out on the bedroll on the floor. He'd almost breathed a sigh of relief when Allison's soft voice came from the sofa.

"Cecelia called. She thinks she's being discharged tomorrow. She has to have an X ray first to make sure her lung stays inflated. But if everything's okay, her doctor says she can go home. I thought I'd ask Gloria to ride along with me."

"I'll take you."

"I don't want to interrupt your work."

"This is part of my work. What about her husband? Is he with her yet?" There was something very intimate about talking in the dark, and he found himself tuned in to every nuance of Allison's voice.

"He arrived today, very distraught about the whole thing. He wanted to come get Pablo but didn't feel he could leave Cecelia. I told her to tell him not to worry, that Pablo was doing well here and he'd be fine for another night."

"He's happy because you've taken good care of him."

"*We've* taken good care of him."

The fan kept the air circulating in the almost silence. Jase had shifted to his side when he heard Allison again.

"Where did you go tonight, Jase?"

"The Cantina."

"Oh."

He couldn't tell if that one syllable carried judgment in it or disappointment. An inner voice said, *Tell her you had a soda with a friend. Tell her about the invitation to Frank's ranch.* But he didn't, and he wasn't sure why. Maybe because he knew whatever she was thinking would keep more distance between them, and that was what he wanted right now.

"Do you date as much as you used to?" she asked.

He didn't, and he couldn't and wouldn't lie to her about that. Over the past year, he'd found he preferred sleeping alone to sleeping with a stranger. "Getting older makes a man more selective," he answered her.

"I see."

But he was sure she didn't see. He was sure she didn't see how she was wrapping his life in turmoil, and how he was questioning every aspect of it. Questioning it didn't mean he wanted to change it. Questioning it didn't mean he'd find any answers, either. The older he got, the fewer answers he found.

Now he wished he'd never returned to Richmond for his niece's christening. If he hadn't, Allison wouldn't be here mucking up his life.

Neither of them said good-night, and as Jase lay there counting each breath, he wondered if he was trying to drive Allison away. Wouldn't that be best for both of them?

When Allison and Jase arrived at the hospital in Albuquerque the next day, they rode up to the surgical wing in the elevator. Allison was carrying Pablo while Jase had the diaper bag and a shopping bag filled with all the things they'd bought but hadn't used. Last night she hadn't slept much. The tension between her and Jase had accumulated into a mountain she couldn't seem to climb. His mood today was remote, and she couldn't seem to break through it. Her attempts at conversation were met with one-word answers and, since she didn't want to babble on all by herself, she'd finally kept quiet except to talk to the baby.

They reached the semiprivate room where Cecelia was recuperating. The second bed in the room was empty. When the woman saw her child, her face lit up and her eyes grew teary.

There was a man sitting beside her who stood when they walked in. Allison carried the baby over to Cecelia and sat him on the bed beside her.

"Oh, thank you," Cecelia said. "I don't know how to repay you for taking care of him for us. We owe you so much."

Both Allison and Jase started to say at the same time, "You don't owe us anything." They exchanged a look, and then Jase lifted the shopping bag. "These are a few extras we had left over."

Cecelia waved to her husband. "Sheriff McGraw, this is my husband, George. George, Sheriff McGraw and Mrs. Rhodes."

"Allison," Allison said softly.

The man came forward to shake her hand and then Jase's.

George's Native American heritage was prominent in the contours of his face, his black hair and eyes. "As my wife said, we can never thank you enough. I insist on paying you for your time and all the supplies you bought."

"No way," Jase said.

"Now look, Sheriff McGraw…"

Jase nodded to the hallway. "Why don't we go out here and talk about it."

Cecelia's arm had gone around Pablo, and she leaned down to kiss his forehead.

As the men left, Allison warned, "You'll have to be careful about lifting him."

"I know. And George won't let me overdo. He's taken a week's vacation. Actually, I think he's worried about driving me home. It will be a three-hour trip. But I told him I'd be fine. Hopefully, Pablo will sleep."

Jase peeked into the room for a moment. "We're going to take these things down to the car." His gaze fell on Allison. "Would you like a drink or anything from the cafeteria? George is going to get some beverages for their trip home."

"Some juice if they have it."

He nodded. "I won't be too long."

Cecelia looked at Allison with questions in her eyes. "So you and Sheriff McGraw are friends?"

"Yes. I'm sort of on a vacation, visiting him."

"I see."

Allison guessed Cecelia was being polite by not saying more. For some reason Allison felt she should explain. "We've known each other for a very long time. He was my husband's best friend. My husband died about a year ago."

Cecelia nodded knowingly. "There's something in the way he looks at you. That's why I asked."

"What do you mean there's something in the way he looks at me?"

After thinking about it for a moment, Cecelia decided, "It's the way a man looks at a woman when he wants her for his own."

Could Cecelia really see that? Could others? Was the attraction between them so evident? "Jase and I are very different. And I...I'm not sure exactly what I want." When she was with Jase and in the moment, she was so drawn to him she couldn't think straight. Yet another part of her told her she could never trust a man again, not after what Dave had done to her.

"It's always complicated between men and women," Cecelia sighed.

"How long have you been married?"

"Three years. And now George and I realize how much we have. After the accident, I was afraid I'd die and never see him or Pablo again. He was so worried he couldn't get back here in time in case something happened. This accident taught us to hold on to each other even stronger. Love is too precious not to enjoy absolutely every minute of it."

Half an hour later, Jase and Allison were riding the elevator down to the lobby, and Allison remembered Cecelia's words. But she attempted conversation about something safer. "I'm going to miss Pablo."

"I know what you mean." Jase's tone was sober.

As the silence lengthened, Allison finally ventured, "I've been thinking about something." The elevator came to a stop and they stepped off. Once the doors closed behind them, she went on, "If I'm going to stay, maybe I should get a room somewhere."

"Is that what you want to do?"

She could hide from Jase as she'd always done or she could be blatantly honest with him and see what happened. "No, I don't particularly want to do that. But I think it might be best."

After a few long moments, he asked, "Because I've been such a bear?"

"No. Because you're not used to having someone

else around. It's not fair for me to take advantage of your hospitality.''

After a few moments, he looked deep into her eyes. "I might be used to living alone, but that doesn't mean it's good for me. A man can get pretty selfish when he has nobody else to consider.''

"You're not selfish, Jase.''

He gave her a wry grimace. "Then you don't know the real me, and maybe you don't want to. But I *would* like you to stay with me while you're here.''

She could tell he meant it, and she could tell something else, too. A bond was forming between them, especially since they'd taken care of Pablo together. The idea should scare her. It did some, but she was more intrigued by it than scared.

She knew she should pack up her bags and leave. She knew she should take one last long look at Red Bluff and say goodbye to the scenery and to Jase. But she couldn't. Not just yet. "If I stay with you a while longer, I have a condition.''

"What condition?" he asked warily.

"We take turns sleeping on the floor.''

"Allison...''

"Those are my terms, Jase.''

Suddenly he shook his head and smiled at her, a smile that made everything inside her go weak. "All right. And maybe we'll get rain soon and the temperatures will cool down. Then we can both sleep in beds.''

The funny thing was, even though that would be more comfortable, Allison would miss sleeping in the same room as Jase.

A little voice inside warned her, *You're going to get hurt. Pack up and leave now.*

But she returned Jase's smile and walked across the lobby with him into the bright sunshine. She'd spend more time considering the warning...later.

Chapter Six

When Allison awakened Saturday morning, she felt disoriented. It was later than usual and, as she looked at the clock on the top of the TV, she saw it was ten o'clock. All of her sleepless nights had apparently caught up with her. Jase had insisted on getting an air mattress for her to use when she slept on the floor. She'd been surprisingly comfortable her second night there. Once Jase had realized she was serious about alternating between the sofa and the floor, he hadn't argued with her about it again.

Sitting up, she realized she must have been in a deep sleep not to have heard Jase leave this morning. Before they'd turned in last night, he'd told her he had a meeting in Albuquerque today. Maybe this afternoon, she'd go shopping for the shorty pajamas she wanted.

After she showered and dressed, she went to the kitchen and saw the note lying on the table. When she picked it up, she read,

Allison—
There's a party tonight at Chuck and Rita's for
Clara's birthday. If you want to go, we won't
have to cook dinner. I should be home by six.

Jase

A birthday party. That sounded like fun. Maybe she
could find something with a Southwest flair to wear
tonight. The two sundresses she'd brought were very
Eastern, very…proper. Suddenly she wanted something not quite so proper, something casually femi-
nine, something different.

She found it that afternoon at a small boutique in
Red Bluff, and when she dressed that evening before
Jase came home, she liked what she saw. She'd
bought a turquoise, gauzy skirt and blouse. The
blouse had puffed sleeves and a scooped neck that
fell softly over her shoulders if she moved too fast.
The front of the blouse was smocked with red and
yellow and white stitching. She'd also found a leather
and silver belt to attach around her waist, dressing up
the outfit a bit, and a Hopi necklace in onyx, mother-
of-pearl and turquoise that looked perfect with everything else. Matching earrings swung from her ears.

She'd swept her hair into a bed of curls on top of
her head and was patting the last wave into place
when she heard Jase come in from the garage. After
slipping into her sandals, she met him in the hall.

He stopped short when he saw her. In his sheriff's
uniform, she didn't think he'd ever looked more
handsome or more powerful. But the way he was staring at her, she wondered if maybe she didn't have a
little bit of power, too.

"Do you like it?" she asked as his gaze passed

from her hair, over her necklace, down her long skirt to her sandals.

"That doesn't look like something you brought from Richmond."

"I went shopping this afternoon." She twirled and the full skirt billowed around her. "What do you think?"

"I think…" He stopped. "I think you look different."

"Different how?" She almost felt as if she was flirting with him.

"Different…freer."

"I felt like a change. What time do you want to leave?"

"Leave?"

"The party," she reminded him.

As if he was trying to focus on the conversation rather than her, he said, "Right. Clara's party." Then he checked his watch. "Give me fifteen minutes to shower and change, then we can go."

As he started to move past her down the hall, she clasped his arm. Their gazes met, and his was filled with a deep intensity that made her release him. Still she asked, "How was your meeting?"

The hall was hot from the heat of the day, and no air was stirring. Jase's male scent mingled with her perfume. She could hear the pounding beat of her heart and wondered if Jase's was pounding as fast.

"Boring," he said in answer to her question. "It was about new forms and regulations and changes we should make in the upcoming year. Now I get to have a meeting with my deputies and go through it all over again."

"While I was shopping today, I bought Clara an

aromatherapy kit with bath oil and perfume and a scented candle. Do you think that's okay?"

"The same scent you use?" he asked, his voice going deeper and huskier.

As he gazed into her eyes, she almost felt dizzy, felt as if the words they were sharing were the surface of something so much deeper. "No," she answered almost breathlessly. "What I wear is much lighter. I bought Clara something a little more exotic."

"I see." He cleared his throat. "She'll probably appreciate it more than the gift certificate from the Cantina I got her."

"I'm sure she'll appreciate that, too."

An aware silence vibrated between them until finally Jase said, "Fifteen minutes and I'll be ready." Then he disappeared into his room.

Allison was in a light mood as Jase parked at the edge of Rita and Chuck's yard along with all the other cars.

"I guess it's not a surprise party," Allison remarked as she heard music playing from behind the house.

"Keeping anything from Clara would be impossible." He climbed out of his truck and came around to Allison's side just as she was getting out.

But when she stepped down, her sandal slipped on the crushed rock lining the curb. She would have fallen, except Jase's strong arms circled her waist and she was suddenly pulled against his chest. When she looked up at him, her heart raced beyond control, and the gold light in his eyes seemed more consuming than any fire she'd ever gone near.

"Are you all right?" he asked.

"I'm fine." She felt short of breath again and knew it wasn't the altitude.

As he released her, he said, "We might as well just go around back."

Landscaping in New Mexico was so different. Large gray, black and reddish rocks were scattered in the yard among the brush. Straggly evergreens edged the side of the house. Allison watched her step as she walked, sneaking a quick glance at Jase. He'd dressed in khaki shorts and a tan polo shirt. The buttons were open at his collar and brown hair curled there. It was getting harder and harder for her to keep her distance from him. It was getting harder and harder to remember the reason she should. Tonight, Richmond and Dave and her marriage seemed very far away, and all she could think about was the way Jase had looked at her...as if he thought she was pretty...as if he really wanted her.

For the past year, she'd wondered when Dave had stopped wanting her...she wondered what had made him stop. But tonight she didn't want to think about any of that.

The party was in full swing, a few couples dancing to the music on the patio. Most of the guests were eating. Clara was sitting at the end of a long redwood table and she waved at Jase and Allison.

Rita came over to them with a wide smile. "I'm glad you could make it. We've got plenty of food." She glanced at the present that Allison was holding. "Do you want me to put that over on the table with the others?"

Allison let Rita take the package and, when the hostess had stepped away, she asked Jase, "Do you want to mingle a while, or get something to eat?"

"Let's get something to eat. It's been a long time since lunch."

They wished Clara a happy birthday, then loaded their plates before they settled in two lawn chairs near the edge of the patio.

A few minutes later, Chuck came over to them and Jase introduced his deputy to Allison. Holding a long-necked bottle of beer, Chuck sank into the chair next to Jase. "Rita's run me ragged today getting ready for this," he said with a grin.

Chuck was shorter than Jase and his sandy-brown hair was longer. She suddenly realized that anytime she saw a man now, she compared him to Jase.

Chuck took a swig of his beer. "Long meeting today?"

"Long enough. We'll have a powwow on Monday and talk about it. Anything happen today I should know about?"

"Wyatt told me while he was on duty, Todd Clemens brought his son by to pay the first installment of the fine you laid on him."

"Todd's son was the ringleader of the boys setting off the firecrackers," Jase explained to Allison so she wasn't cut out of the conversation.

"He made his son get a job at the new burger joint to pay it off," Chuck went on. "He surprised me when he said he was glad you didn't let him off easy."

"They could have been maimed or worse," Jase said gruffly. "I was tempted to let Todd junior sit in a cell for the night."

"Why didn't you?" his deputy asked him.

"Couple of reasons." But Jase didn't go into them. Instead he took a bite of his hamburger.

Rita beckoned to her husband and he said, "Uh-oh, duty calls."

After Chuck had crossed the patio, Allison asked Jase, "You really would have put a teenager in a cell for the night?"

"I might have. But he seemed scared enough. If Clark Rhodes hadn't done that to me, I don't know where I'd be right now."

Clark Rhodes was her father-in-law. He, too, was a police officer and Allison had always suspected that Jase had become a cop to emulate the man he'd taken as his role model. During the time Jase had spent around Dave's house, Clark had almost become a surrogate father.

"How old were you?" she asked.

"Seventeen. It was over Christmas vacation that year. I'd gone out looking for trouble with—" He stopped. "With a couple of guys. Someone had brought along a fifth of vodka and we had more false courage than common sense. We hot-wired a car and took it for a joyride."

Allison had heard things about Jase while she was dating Dave, about his penchant for trouble. But she hadn't known how much of it was true. "What happened?"

"We landed in a ditch and couldn't get it going again. The car belonged to Bob Case's dad. Someone called the police, and Bob and I were taken down to the station. Bob's father promised to take care of *him*. At that point, my mother didn't know what to do with me and I didn't have anybody who cared what she *did* do with me. So Clark Rhodes decided he'd show me what life on the wild side really looked like. He left me in jail for the night."

When Jase closed his eyes and his face took on such a sober expression, she knew he was reliving it. "I'll never forget the eerie, trapped feel of the place," he went on. "The next day Mr. Rhodes took me to the state prison. He had the warden show me up and down the cells. He even sat me in one and said if I didn't straighten out, that's where I'd end up. He wanted to know if that's the kind of future I wanted."

"That was awfully harsh," Allison protested.

"Maybe. But it did the trick. That day I decided I wanted a real future, not one where someone else had control of my life."

"Is that when you decided to become a police officer?"

"Not exactly. But after looking around at my choices, it seemed the best option. Besides, I saw it as a way I could make a difference."

It was ironic. Allison wasn't sure her husband had thought about being a police officer in that way. She'd gotten the feeling he'd done it because it was more or less expected of him, and he'd seen it as a way to make his father proud of him. He'd also liked the authority his uniform had given him. With Jase, power and authority didn't seem to be any part of it. He exuded those, but she felt more, too. He had a strong code of honor. She also felt protecting others came naturally to him. He did want to do a good job and, as he'd said, make a difference.

"Are you thinking about Dave?" Jase asked gruffly.

She just nodded, not able to explain that she admired him more than she'd ever admired her husband.

As Jase tried to finish eating, the anger that rose up in him made swallowing difficult. He shouldn't *be*

angry. Allison had every right to think about Dave as
often as she wanted. But dammit, she shouldn't look
so pretty tonight.

He realized he was thinking irrationally, but he
couldn't seem to do anything about it. Then he wondered if he was angry merely at Allison.

He still remembered that night when he and Bob
and *Dave* had hot-wired that car. Dave had had more
to drink than any of them and had enthusiastically
gone along with the whole prank. Since it was Bob's
father's car, they hadn't officially stolen it. But Bob
hadn't had permission to use it and that was just as
bad. The thing was, when they'd driven into that
ditch, Dave had panicked. He said he couldn't be
caught there with them and it would ruin his future.
He'd pleaded with them not to rat on him. He should
have known they wouldn't. They were his friends.

So he'd run off, and no one had ever known he'd
been with them that night.

But Dave had been a good cop and apparently a
wonderful husband from the way Allison was grieving. He remembered the package in his pocket he intended to give to her. Maybe later. Maybe when the
sadness left her eyes.

Allison mingled after they'd finished eating. She
was so good with people. She could talk to anyone.
It was probably because she listened so well. It made
talking to her very easy.

All of the guests watched Clara open her gifts. The
dispatcher seemed overwhelmed by everybody's
thoughtfulness, especially Virgil's when he gave her
a pair of dangling sterling silver earrings and a five-
pound box of chocolates. "I might let you have one
or two," she'd teased after she'd pulled off the ear-

rings she was wearing to attach the new ones to her ears.

Jase watched Virgil and Clara closely as they sat together to eat cake and ice cream, and he realized a romance was blossoming in the sheriff's office. Who would have thought?

Music coming from the CD player was lively. Allison sat on the fringe of the patio at first, then one of Jase's younger deputies, Rod Coolridge, asked her to try the Texas two-step with him. She did and looked as if she was having a hell of a lot of fun doing it. Then she danced with another deputy, Wyatt Baumgardner.

But Jase remembered the torture of dancing with her in the Cantina the night she'd arrived, holding her close but not being able to do enough about it. They were both better off if she danced with everyone but him. The problem was, he didn't like another man having his arms around her. He didn't like her having so much fun with someone else. His mood grew blacker by the minute.

Finally around eleven, the guests started leaving. He tapped her shoulder to see if she was ready to go, and her bare skin under his fingers made his voice gruff. "I'm ready whenever you are."

Looking up at him, she said, "Just let me get my purse."

They wished Clara a happy birthday once more and said goodbye to everyone, then went to Jase's truck. He opened the door for her, and she climbed inside. After he'd gotten in, he felt like slamming the door. But he didn't. He knew how to control frustration and anger and every other emotion that came along. He'd been doing it all his life.

The air was a bit cooler as the temperature dropped to the seventies. Jase left his window open and so did Allison. It tousled her upswept hair, threatening to loosen it. He'd like to loosen it. He'd like to let it run through his fingers while he kissed her.

Trying to get his mind onto anything else, he remembered Frank Nightwalker's invitation. "How would you like to go riding tomorrow?"

He could almost feel her turn toward him. He could almost feel her eyes on him. "Where?"

"There's a man I know—Frank Nightwalker. He has a ranch a few miles out. I've gone riding there before. He invited us over tomorrow for supper and then riding afterward if we'd like."

"That was nice of him."

"His father lived with him, but since he died over a year ago, Frank's kept to himself a lot. I think he just wants some company."

"He sounds like Gloria."

"Frank's a lot quieter."

Allison laughed, and Jase loved the sound of it. "So do you want to go?"

She nodded. "Yes, it sounds like fun. I think I'm going to go to church in the morning, though. Would you like to come along?"

"I'll pass. There are some things I want to do around the house and I don't have enough time to do them." He should have guessed Allison was the churchgoing type. His sense of a connection outside of himself came from perching on one of the bluffs to watch the sunrise and feel a power greater than he'd ever felt among men.

Once they were back in Jase's kitchen, he felt for the box in his shorts pocket. Slipping the present from his pocket, he held it out to her. "I got you something today."

Her eyes were wide and beaming with a question that she asked. "Why?"

"It's just a memento of your visit. I had time on my lunch hour."

Taking the box from him, she untied the white bow and then tore off the gold foil. When she lifted the lid, she exclaimed, "Oh, it's the barrette I liked." Carefully she took it out of the box and ran her thumb over the stones, appreciating the agate and turquoise. "It's beautiful, Jase. Thank you."

She looked genuinely pleased, and he was glad he'd bought it. "Do you want to see how it looks?" he asked.

"Oh, but my hair's up…"

"I can remedy that." When he moved closer to her, her eyes widened in surprise, and when his hands went to her hair, he thought she might move away. But she didn't. She stood very still.

"I don't want to hurt you," he said, finding the large hair clip and running his thumb over it to see how it worked.

"You won't."

She seemed a lot more sure of that than he was. He loved the feel of her hair under his fingers, and he didn't open the clip right away as his fingertips brushed through the silkiness. There was one main clip and a few other pins. As her hair began to fall and he stroked through the strands, he thought she trembled. But it could have been his imagination. He could just want her to like his touch.

Finally he released the last pin. As her hair fell in a beautiful golden cloud of silk around her face, he combed his fingers through it, and she closed her eyes.

Then he said, "Let me have the barrette."

Looking up at him, she handed it to him. Her cheeks were a bit flushed, and he could see the pulse at her throat beating in the rhythm of his own heart.

Slipping the barrette above her temple, he let it capture a few locks. When he was finished, he rested his hands on her shoulders. "It's just right."

The way she was looking up at him made his heart pound.

He was drawing her closer when the scanner on the counter erupted into a series of calls. Allison tensed under his hands and he sucked in a breath, listening in spite of himself. He heard all available units being mobilized because of a burglary, and when his phone rang he snatched it up. "McGraw."

Allison moved farther away from Jase, away from the attraction she felt for him. She heard him say, "Yeah, I heard the code. Who's on the scene? Don't let anyone touch anything. I'll be there in ten minutes."

When he hung up, she asked, "What is it?"

"A burglary. Two miles west of town. I've got to get over there."

Overwhelming fear gripped Allison. As Jase went to the front door to head for the sheriff's vehicle parked at the curb, she called his name.

He stopped at the door and waited.

"Please be careful," she said, wanting to say so much more.

"I always am."

Then he was gone and her fingers went to the barrette in her hair, remembering the feel of his hands as he'd stroked through it. Heaven help her, she was in love with Jase McGraw and she didn't know what to do about it.

The living room seemed terrifically warm tonight, even with the fan running. Changing into her new shorty pajamas, she readied herself for bed. But she knew she wouldn't be able to sleep. She'd stowed Jase's bedroll along with the air mattress into a corner of the living room and now she arranged both on the floor, thumping his pillow, making sure the sheet on the bedroll was smooth. There was a ball of anxiety inside of her that she couldn't wish away. She certainly couldn't reason it away. Reason told her police officers were always in danger and that included tough sheriffs. The messages on the scanner had calmed down and she wasn't learning anything from it, though she'd turned it up to make sure she could hear it.

Then she waited.

She tried to read, but couldn't. Rearranging the fan, hoping it would circulate cooler air from somewhere, she tried to watch TV but couldn't concentrate on that, either. She'd brought a crossword puzzle magazine along on the plane, but the letters danced in front of her eyes and the words made no sense. What if the burglar was still around? What if he had a gun? She'd seen Jase's gun in his shoulder holster. She knew he usually kept it locked in the glove compartment of the sheriff's SUV. Did he ever have to use it?

She hated the waiting. She'd hated waiting for Dave and she couldn't imagine having to do it again. She couldn't be in love with another lawman. She couldn't be in love. She'd been here less than two weeks!

But then she thought about the christening and all the years before.

By the light beside the sofa, she tried again to read, but when Jase came in, she jumped up from the cushions and ran into the kitchen to him. "Are you okay?"

He looked tired, and when his gaze passed over her pajama set, it drifted down her legs to her feet. She probably should have put a robe on, but it was so blasted hot and the cotton wasn't see-through.

"I'm fine. I guess you got that outfit the same place you got the dress."

"Yes, but—" She wasn't going to get sidetracked by talking about what she was wearing. "What happened?"

Crossing to the kitchen windowsill, he dropped his keys there. "Nothing happened. There's been a series of burglaries on the outskirts of Albuquerque and surrounding towns. We dusted for prints, and I talked to a neighbor who'd seen two men in a gray truck cruising around the area."

He stopped suddenly, searching her face, noticing her clasped hands, her fingers interlocked with tension. "Allison, I wasn't in any danger. The burglary happened while the couple was out. The burglars were long gone."

"Why do police officers think that if there isn't a gun pointed at them, they're not in danger? Dave used to tell me that all the time and look what happened to him!"

Moving closer to her again, Jase said in a low

voice, "This isn't Richmond, it's Red Bluff, New Mexico. We have a very low crime rate."

"So low," she murmured, "that you just returned from the scene of a burglary." In spite of herself, the tension of waiting for the past hour and a half caused tears to burn in her eyes. She turned away and went into the living room.

But Jase followed her. "Don't worry about me, Allison. I'll stay safe."

"You can't promise that." To her embarrassment, her voice broke.

Jase caught her arm and drew her around to face him. His hand came up to caress her cheek, and the look in his eyes... When his lips came down to meet hers, she didn't care about yesterday or tomorrow. All she cared about was now.

The kiss took on a life of its own. At first it was sweet, then hard and demanding. She met Jase's demand standing on tiptoe, lacing her hands into his hair. But then their desire overflowed the kiss. Their lips and tongues weren't enough. They both wanted more. Jase touched her first, lifting her short cotton top, pressing his hand to her breast. It was as if he'd lit a fuse and she felt like a firecracker ready to pop. She wanted to feel his skin, his chest hair, his shoulders, his back, *all* of him. And she couldn't seem to do it fast enough. Pulling his shirt from his shorts, she ran her hands up his chest, and he groaned.

She wasn't sure when they sank down onto the bedroll. They did it in one motion, never breaking the kiss. Jase tore away for a second to toss his shirt over his head as she reached for the snap on his shorts. Then he was on top of her on the bedroll. The world was spinning, the heat was becoming steam, and all she could think about was Jase filling her world. His knee separated her legs and then he was lifting her top over her head. When he kissed her again, she arched against his knee wantonly.

He swore and growled, "Allison, you're making me crazy." His lips were on her neck, her shoulders, and then her breasts. She clutched at him, eager for him to kiss her everywhere.

But suddenly Jase stopped and broke away. He was breathing raggedly and his eyes were filled with the passion they were sharing. "Are you sure about this? Are you sure you won't have regrets?"

The word *regrets* echoed in her head like a loud, painful bell.

What was she doing? What were *they* doing? Did Jase want her for her, or did he just need a woman? Any woman. He'd said he couldn't settle down, and even more than that, could she *trust* him to settle down?

After Dave's betrayal, she didn't know if she could trust any man.

Mortified at what she'd gotten herself into, embarrassed because they were both in such a state, she grabbed her top and held it in front of her.

His voice was deep and filled with frustration as he stated, "I guess you just gave me my answer."

Chapter Seven

Allison sat in church the next morning, trying to make sense of everything that had happened over the past year. The church had been half-filled during the service and now she was the only one who'd lingered, sitting in the silence, looking for answers.

Dave's death had seemed so senseless, and she'd hardly absorbed the shock of it when she'd found the letters. In a matter of minutes, her grief had been disturbed by a raw sense of betrayal that had haunted her every waking minute as well as her sleep-filled ones.

When she *could* sleep. When she wasn't questioning. When she wasn't analyzing what she'd done wrong.

What had happened to her marriage? Why hadn't she seen that Dave was unhappy? Why hadn't she noticed the signs that he'd turned to someone else: the hours he'd been "working" long past his shifts, his new casual wardrobe, his evasive mumblings when she walked in on a phone conversation he hastily terminated? He'd told her the department was shorthanded. He'd told her his off-duty clothes were out of style. He'd told her they'd gotten a lot of wrong numbers lately. He was her husband, and she'd never doubted him. She'd believed in their marriage.

But Dave's betrayal had shattered her ability to trust.

What had she been trying to do last night, getting dressed up like that, needing Jase to look at her as if she was a woman he wanted? Was she trying to get back at Dave with his best friend?

No. That answer was too easy. Jase had become *her* friend now, not Dave's. He'd become so much more. Yet she couldn't let him be more. She couldn't trust him to be more.

And Jase McGraw didn't want more. He claimed he didn't know anything about settling down, about one-man-one-woman relationships, about marriage being a forever union.

So how and why had she let herself fall in love with him?

In the silence, she couldn't find the answers.

Last night, as she'd clutched her shorty pajama top to her in embarrassment, Jase had sworn, muttered something about knowing better, then left her in the living room alone. Shaken, she'd put on her top, turned out the light and sat on the corner of the sofa trying to fight back the tears. She'd heard the shower running, and she'd braced herself for Jase's anger as he'd come back into the living room and stretched out on his bedroll.

Knowing probably neither of them could sleep until they cleared the air, she'd asked, "Jase?"

But he'd said in a clipped tone, "Go to sleep, Allison."

She'd known what that meant. He didn't want to talk about it. He wasn't going to talk about it.

This morning she'd heard him get up, but he'd gone outside before she was dressed. When she'd left for church, he was replacing one of the timbers in his split-rail fence.

Picking up her purse from the pew, Allison decided she couldn't postpone the inevitable. She had to go back to Jase's house and try to talk to him about last night.

But after she returned to the ranch house, he was still working outside. She watched from the kitchen window as he picked up cottonwood boughs that had fallen from a hollowed-out tree. Circles of sweat stained his shirt. She didn't know how long she watched him from the window. His movements were efficient and purposeful. The brim of his hat shaded his face, but she knew his rugged features by heart. Even when she closed her eyes, she could see his face clearly.

When he carried his tools to the shed out back, she knew he was finished. The thought of him coming inside sent her pulse racing. A few minutes later when he came through the garage into the house, she took a pitcher of lemonade she'd made the day before from the refrigerator and poured him a glass.

He glanced at her briefly, washed his hands at the sink and dried them. When he turned toward her, she handed him the glass of lemonade.

He took it and drank it down, then set the glass on the counter. "Thanks."

"Do you want another?"

"No, not right now." Taking off his hat, he hung it on the rack near the door and ran his hand through his hair. "Do you still want to go out to Frank's later?"

"Do you?"

He studied her for a long moment. "It might be best. Spending time alone together isn't a good idea."

"I'm sorry about last night," she said, meaning it.

"You'd be a lot sorrier if we *hadn't* stopped. It's a good thing we came to our senses."

But she wasn't so sure of that. Part of her still wanted him desperately. Part of her needed to be held in his arms. But she couldn't tell him that. She couldn't tell him so many things.

"I'm going to get some lunch and then wash the truck."

It was awkward around Jase now, and she figured it would be better if she stayed out of his way. "I told Gloria I'd visit with her this afternoon for a while. What time do you want to leave?"

"Around four."

"That's fine. When I went to the store last week, I bought ingredients to make a batch of fudge in the microwave. Do you think Mr. Nightwalker would like that?"

"I'm sure he would."

They didn't talk much after that, and as Allison took packs of lunch meat from the refrigerator, she wondered if she'd ever feel comfortable with Jase again.

Frank Nightwalker welcomed them with a handshake and tall glasses of iced tea. His adobe house was more than comfortable, and the ceiling fan in the vaulted living room was ideal. As they sat there making conversation, Allison began to relax. Maybe because Jase was comfortable with Frank, maybe because a third party acted as a buffer.

After they'd finished their tea, Frank said, "I have the ribs in the slow cooker. They should be finished shortly. Would you like to look around?" he asked Allison.

"I'd love to. I've never been on a ranch before."

He laughed. "I think you call them farms back east, but as Jase knows, I can't wait to show you my prize bull. He's revitalized my herd, so I like to show him off."

Allison had heard stories about bulls. "Isn't he dangerous?"

Frank's high cheekbones rose as he gave her a wide grin. "Come see for yourself."

As they'd sat and talked, Allison had noticed Frank was favoring his right arm, but his long shirtsleeve covered anything that might have been there. The hot wind whipped around them as Frank led them to the corral behind the barn. Allison shaded her eyes against the sun, scanning the ranch land as far as she could see. The landscape was dotted with cactus, sage and cottonwood.

At her elbow, Jase admitted, "I'd like to have a place like this someday."

Frank's gaze was thoughtful as it rested on Jase. "I've been thinking about selling off some of my land. It's more than I need and more than I want. Would you like to know when I decide to do it?"

"I was thinking about a few years down the road," Jase responded.

"It could appreciate in value until then," Frank offered with a wink.

"It doesn't sound as if you'll ever come back to Richmond." Allison wanted to know where Jase's life was headed and if their paths would cross after she left.

"Not likely," Jase said with a shrug. "My life's here now."

And hers wasn't. Everything she'd known all her life was back in Richmond.

Frank took them around to the back of the barn and into one of the corrals. Allison hesitantly hung back when she saw the huge white animal with a gold ring in his nose.

"Maybe you'd appreciate him better with a fence between you. Go around on the outside of the fence. I'll bring him over."

Jase followed Allison outside the length of fence until they reached the proximity of the bull. Then Frank put his hand on the bull's neck and nudged him over to where they stood. There he looked at Allison and scratched the bull between the ears. "This is Bucko, and he says it's a pleasure to meet you. You can scratch him up here on the head if you want."

Still unsure, but not wanting to seem like a coward, she put her hand through the fence rails and scratched the animal between his ears. He moved forward and she backed up. But then she realized, he just wanted her to scratch longer and harder.

She laughed. "You're not going to tell me he's as gentle as a pet."

"Lord, no! He's got wildness in him just like all the critters we try to tame," Frank concluded, tilting up the brim of his Stetson. "He's big, and that scares some folks. He seems tough. But just like a lot of men, he's not so tough under the right hand." Frank's almost black eyes danced over her and then over to Jase.

She got the obvious message, sure Jase probably had, too. Was Jase just tough on the outside? What did he feel for her? Could she tame him?

That idea was ridiculous. If she hadn't been able to hold on to Dave, she certainly wouldn't be able to handle a man like Jase. He was used to lots of women, probably beautiful women, who were freer and tons more experienced than she was.

Continuing the tour, Frank took them through the barn then, pointing out the two horses Jase would probably want to saddle to take Allison riding.

Jase glanced around the barn. "You've got a really nice place here, Frank."

"I think so. It's just a shame I..." The older man stopped. "I built it up as a legacy, hoping someday my children would come looking for me. But that hasn't happened, and I'd better get used to the idea that it won't."

"You're not in touch with them?" Allison asked.

Frank looked over at Jase. "I see you know how to keep a man's secrets. My tongue was a little too loose the other night," he decided with a wry grimace. Turning once more to Allison, he explained, "It's a long story, but my son and daughter have lives with their mother and grandfather that they're never going to want to leave. God knows what they've told Mac and Suzette about me."

"You could contact them yourself," Allison suggested. "If they're adults."

"My son's about Jase's age, my daughter two years

younger. With the resources at their disposal, they could have found me long ago if they'd wanted to. Nope. When I die, the ranch will be sold and that will be the end of it.'' Frank absently leaned across the stall to pat a bay gelding on the neck, but when he did, he winced as his forearm brushed the top rung.

Allison couldn't keep from commenting. ''I noticed you're favoring your right arm. I'm a nurse. Would you like me to look at it?''

After he studied her for a moment, he rolled up his sleeve. There were three nasty, ragged cuts that had pink around them. They looked as if they were infected. She felt around the scratches and there was heat there. ''How did you do this?''

''Barbed wire. I got careless.''

''Have you had a tetanus shot lately?''

''About two years ago. It'll be fine. It just needs time to heal.''

''If that gets any redder, or you start seeing pink streaks up your arm, you get to the clinic.''

''I'll keep an eye on it,'' Frank muttered. But the way he said it, Allison wasn't sure he would.

Fifteen minutes later, they were sitting in Frank's dining room, eating and chatting like old friends. The ribs were messy but delicious and a corn muffin melted in Allison's mouth. She couldn't help but think Frank Nightwalker's children were missing out on knowing a very interesting man.

The sun was sinking closer to the horizon when Jase led Allison into the barn again later. ''You've been on a horse before, right?''

''I took lessons as a teenager, but I used an English saddle, not a Western one. Does that matter?''

''That depends.''

"On what?"

"How well you take to a Western saddle. It'll feel bouncier. You can't hug the horse with your knees like you do on an English saddle. But I'm sure you'll get the hang of it."

Jase had kept a wide berth around her all day, careful not to get too close. Now was no different. He saddled up the horses and they led them outside. Allison's horse was at least seventeen hands high and, when she inspected the stirrup, she wasn't sure how she was going to swing herself up.

Jase saw her predicament. "I'll give you a lift. Try to get your toe up into the stirrup and hold on to the pommel."

When she did as he directed, he set one large hand at her waist, and she felt his other at the seat of her jeans. Before she could protest, he'd given her a hoist up, and she found herself sitting in the saddle. But she could still feel the brand of his fingers—still remember vividly every moment of their kissing and touching last night.

Jase looked up at her from the ground. "You all right?"

When she gazed into his eyes, she could see that he was remembering, too. Then she lied. "I'm just fine." When he handed her the reins, she took them, careful not to let her fingers touch his.

Then he swung into his saddle as if he'd been doing it all his life. The leather creaked as he settled in and started his horse walking away from the barn. "We'll take it slow to get you used to the saddle. Try to ease into the motion of it."

With her horse walking, she didn't have a problem. But when Jase nudged his horse into a trot and she tried to keep up, she thought she'd bounce right out of the saddle. Pulling on the reins, she slowed her horse to a walk again.

Jase was quite a ways ahead now, and he stopped and turned. "Problem?" he called.

When she reached him, she said, "I'm afraid I'll fall off."

He gave her an assessing look. "Would that be so bad? Wouldn't it be worth feeling the wind in your hair and the speed under you to take a little tumble?"

"I just need a little more time to get used to the saddle." She wasn't a risk taker. Didn't he know that? She didn't like thrills for the sake of thrills, and she couldn't see hurting either her body or her ego without a very good reason.

He blew out a breath. "Okay." He stretched his hand to the north. "We'll walk them over to those cottonwoods by the creek bed. Maybe by then you'll feel more confident."

She knew she was holding him back, and that was the problem with a man like Jase. A woman like her *would* hold him back. He was a take-chances, jump-right-in kind of person. She was usually cautious, mapping out every step.

So why had she flown to Albuquerque on impulse, and why had she let Jase's kiss last night sweep her away? Could she change the way she'd always looked at life?

She was feeling more comfortable in the saddle as they walked the horses along the almost dried up creek bed. They stopped under the trees for a while and just let the wind blow past them, stirring up dust and desire and maybe even future dreams.

Jase gazed out over the land and finally broke the

silence. "When I was a kid living in a trailer park, I never imagined I'd see country like this someday, let alone own a piece of it."

"You really want to live on a ranch?"

"Not a ranch exactly. I'd just like to have a little more land than I do now."

"It's a shame Frank doesn't have someone to share his life with."

He gave her a sideways glance. "You mean a wife?"

"A wife...or his children. I can see that he's built a life that he likes for himself. But when two people build something together, it seems more important. More lasting."

Jase faced her then. "You'd know about that. I wouldn't. Are you ready to head back?"

End of discussion. He didn't want to talk about sharing, or two people building more than they could ever have separately. As far as that went, she didn't even know how much *she* believed in that anymore, either. "I'm ready to head back," she murmured.

Jase kept his horse at a walk in deference to her. But suddenly she decided she could show him she wasn't a coward, that she wanted to feel the wind wrapping around her, that she wanted to taste freedom. Urging her horse into a trot, she gave him his head. At first she tried to post in the saddle, but that was impossible. Finally she found herself in tune with the horse and his rhythm. He broke into a canter and she felt as if she were flying.

Jase was beside her, then slightly ahead of her, glancing over at her every once in a while to make sure she was okay. Finally, when Frank's house came into sight, she slowed her horse to a walk again.

Jase almost smiled at her. "I guess you got the hang of it."

"I guess I did," she said smugly as they walked the horses back to the barn to cool them down.

Outside the barn door, Jase dismounted. She was about to dismount herself when she felt his large hands at her waist, helping her to the ground. She turned into his arms, breathed in his scent and gazed up into his eyes. It seemed as if they stared at each other like that forever until her horse moved, she stepped back, and Jase dropped his arms.

Disconcerted by the sensual pull of him and turmoil from all the feelings he aroused in her, she spun around and grabbed the reins on her horse.

Frank emerged from inside the barn door. "I'll help you groom them. Then how about a game of cards?"

Allison glanced at Jase, realizing once again that Frank was as lonely as Gloria was. She gave a little nod that staying a while longer was fine with her.

Jase answered for them both. "Sure, a game of cards sounds good."

Allison knew being with Frank was easier than the two of them being alone, and so did Jase.

On Monday morning, Allison did laundry, including some of Jase's that she found in the hamper. It seemed extremely intimate handling his clothes. But she liked the feeling. They'd come home last night, gotten ready for bed, said good-night and gone to sleep. She'd insisted on taking her turn on the floor so Jase could have the sofa. He hadn't argued with her.

She supposed Jase had gotten a good night's sleep. She hadn't heard him tossing and turning as she had some other nights. This morning he was up and gone before she could even make coffee.

After she'd hung Jase's shirts on hangers and folded the towels, she remembered the nice evening they'd had last night with Frank Nightwalker. She considered again the cuts on his arm. Those had been ugly, and they hadn't looked as if they were healing. Maybe she'd eat some lunch, then drive out to his place to check on him.

It was around one when she arrived at Frank's ranch, knowing she might be on a wild-goose chase. He might not even be there. But she parked near his house anyway and knocked on the door. No one answered.

Shading her eyes against the sun, she saw a flash of denim near the barn and she headed that way. When she saw him, she immediately became concerned. He was holding a pitchfork but leaning on it heavily. His hat was on the ground and he was sweating profusely.

"What's going on, Frank?"

Looking over at her, he answered, "I'm feeling pretty ragged."

She touched his forehead and could tell he had a fever. Then she took his arm and lifted his sleeve. The pink area had widened around the cuts. She didn't see streaks yet, thank goodness, but it was bad enough. Slipping her arm around him, she said, "Come on, lean on me. I'm taking you to the clinic."

"No, I can't. I have chores."

"The chores are going to have to wait if you fall flat on your face, and that's what's going to happen if you don't take care of this. Now come on, we're going."

He looked down at her, a slip of a smile on his lips. "Didn't know you were so bossy."

"Only now and then."

Once on the highway, Allison tried to keep to the speed limit, but she was worried about Frank and how fast the infection might be spreading.

When they arrived at the clinic, Allison saw Jase's SUV parked there. Was he having lunch with Maria?

Trying to put that out of her mind and keep her attention on Frank, she helped him inside. The waiting room was empty and she saw the sign that said office hours would resume again at three. After she helped Frank to a seat, she went to the receptionist's desk to ask if Maria was in her office. Allison told her what Frank's problem was and the receptionist went to the back.

A few minutes later, the waiting room door opened. Maria took one look at Frank and came over to him. "What did you do now?" she asked good-naturedly.

"Had a fight with some barbed wire. This little lady hog-tied me and made me come with her."

Maria laughed. "That's some feat. Come back with me and we'll get you fixed up."

But when Frank stood, he swayed and both women reached around his waist.

"Now that's the kind of attention I like," he joked.

Maria shook her head. "Tough old coots are the hardest to treat. Don't you agree, Allison?"

"Yep, they rank right up there with two-year-olds," Allison decided as they helped Frank down the hall toward an examining room.

They'd just seated Frank inside on the gurney when Jase came to stand in the doorway. "What's up?"

Frank waved at Allison. "Your lady-friend insisted

I come in here. I got to admit, I wasn't getting much done."

Maria stuck a thermometer in Frank's mouth and then looked at his arm where his sleeve was rolled up. "It's good and infected, Frank. Do you want me to examine you with company or without?"

"It doesn't matter to me," he mumbled around the thermometer.

Suddenly embarrassed and feeling as if she were intruding, not only in Frank's life, but in Maria and Jase's, too, Allison said, "I'll go sit in the waiting room."

But Maria insisted, "There's a couch in my office. Why don't you wait in there? It's more comfortable. I'll give you the verdict after I examine him."

Avoiding Jase's gaze, Allison went to Maria's office but didn't sit on the couch. Rather, she stood at the window looking out.

"I guess you went out to Frank's place," Jase commented from the doorway.

She glanced over her shoulder at him, then looked outside once more. "I was worried. His arm didn't look good yesterday."

She could feel each one of Jase's bootfalls as he came closer. "I'll bet he's glad you did."

"Maybe, maybe not."

Tension was thick in the office.

"What's the matter, Allison?"

What was the matter? She wanted to know why he was here seeing Maria. Were they having lunch? A rendezvous?

But before she could voice any of the questions, Maria came to the doorway. "I'm going to start him on antibiotics. I'll give him an injection. That will get them into his system faster. Then he can go home if he promises to behave himself.''

"Should he be there alone?'' Allison asked.

"Probably not for the next few hours. Once the antibiotics start working, he'll feel a lot better.''

"I'll take him home and stay with him,'' Allison said.

"Are you sure you want to do that?'' Jase asked, his eyes examining her carefully.

"He'll need something light to eat for supper. He's worried about the chores, though. I'd help, but—''

"There's a teenager who helps him,'' Jase said. "But I'll come out after work and do whatever needs to be done. If he's still not feeling well, I can stay the night. That's if you don't mind staying at my place by yourself.''

"That's fine,'' Allison said lightly, actually relieved at the idea. "Maybe we'll both get a good night's sleep for a change.''

It was unlike her to make comments like that, and Maria looked from one of them to the other. "Well, uh…I'm going to get Frank the injection.''

"And I've got to get back to the office,'' Jase said with a speculative look at Allison. When he'd crossed to Maria, Allison asked the doctor, "Are you sure you don't mind if I wait here until Frank's finished?''

"Of course, I don't mind.''

"Allison?'' Jase asked when she wouldn't look at him.

"What?'' Finally her eyes met his.

"I should finish up about six. I'll be out at Frank's soon after.''

"Fine," she responded as if it didn't matter.

Then the beautiful doctor and Jase were walking down the hall, leaving Allison alone with her thoughts.

Chapter Eight

When Gloria came to the door the next day, Allison was making sandwiches to take to Frank. Last night after Jase had arrived at Frank's ranch, she'd made them all supper and then stuck around until Jase had fed the horses and done a few chores around the barn. Afterward she'd come back here. She and Jase hadn't talked much to each other, just concentrated on taking care of Frank. This morning Jase had called to tell her Frank was feeling better and was practically kicking him out, saying he didn't need a baby-sitter.

Frank might not need a baby-sitter, but she wanted to make sure he was okay. Taking him lunch was a good excuse to stop by and make sure.

She went to the door and smiled at Gloria. "Hi, there. I was just on my way out."

"I brought you some of that peach marmalade I told you about," Gloria said, holding up the jar.

"Come on in." Allison could talk to Gloria as she finished up the sandwiches.

As Gloria trailed her into the kitchen, the older woman said, "I heard you come back last night, but I never heard Jase's truck."

Spreading mustard on bread, Allison explained as she worked, telling her neighbor what had happened to Frank and that Jase had stayed the night.

"What a nice thing to do," Gloria said. "I guess Frank's like me and doesn't have anybody nearby to help him out. I've spoken to him a couple of times at community to-dos. He's always been pleasant." The older woman set the marmalade on the counter. "I can see you're busy and want to get going. I won't hold you up."

Allison genuinely enjoyed talking to Gloria in spite of what Jase had said about her being a gossip. Allison wasn't sure she was. Gloria might keep her ear to the ground to make sure she knew all the latest news, but Allison wasn't so sure she helped spread it.

"Stay and talk to me while I finish here. Would you like a cup of coffee? I made some earlier."

Giving her a wide, pleased smile, Gloria sat at the kitchen table. "That'd be great."

After Allison had poured her a cup and set it on the table, Gloria asked, "Are you going to the town council meeting tonight?"

"I didn't know there was one."

"Oh, yes. Second Tuesday of every month. Jase will be going. As sheriff he's part of the council."

"I see. And it's open to the public?"

"Mmm-hmm. Anyone can bring up anything that's on their mind, and the mayor and council listen. It keeps folks from grumbling among themselves."

"I guess it might. Will you be going?"

"I wouldn't miss it."

Allison laughed. "Maybe I'll tag along with Jase and see you there."

For the next few minutes, as Allison finished making the sandwiches, she and Gloria talked about Red Bluff and a little bit of everything else, too. Then Gloria left, saying she'd see her tonight.

When Allison arrived at Frank's, he was looking much better. She insisted on taking his temperature, and he grumbled that everyone was making too much of a fuss. But he let her. It was only slightly elevated now, and as she ate lunch with him, she was sure he was on the mend. Before she left, she warned him not to overdo and he assured her he had someone coming to help with the chores.

As Allison left the ranch, she thought about how much she liked the rancher. He reminded her of her father.

That evening when Jase came home, she was fixing a salad to go with the hamburgers sizzling on the patio grill. She'd already dressed for the council meeting in pale pink slacks and a white-and-pink-striped sleeveless blouse.

Jase's brows arched when he saw her. "Going out tonight?"

"Gloria told me about the town council meeting."

"You'll be bored," Jase said matter-of-factly, hanging his hat on the rack at the door.

"I think it will be interesting to see how a small town operates. I can drive myself if you have to go early."

"I don't have to go early."

"Then is it okay if I tag along?"

"Sure. We meet in the cafeteria at the elementary school. Did you go out to Frank's today?"

"He's doing fine. He said he had someone to help him with his chores and we weren't supposed to worry about him. But I told him I'd call him tomorrow anyway."

Jase loosened his bolo tie, slipped it over his head and set it on the counter. "I can tell he isn't used to having someone help him out."

"Everyone needs help now and then." She realized that if she hadn't seen Jase when he came to Richmond, she'd still be working, absorbed in the turmoil of the past year, not really enjoying life.

"Sometimes it's hard for a man to accept help," Jase admitted.

"All that male pride?" she asked in a teasing voice, trying to lighten the atmosphere between them.

He gave her a crooked smile in return. "I suppose so."

His gaze seemed to swallow her as they stood there, and she could remember the feel of his strong arms around her, the feel of his lips on hers.

He broke the moment, deliberately she guessed, by asking, "Do I have enough time before supper to change into a clean shirt?"

"Sure, go ahead."

As Jase left the kitchen, all Allison could think about was the vision of him shirtless, his broad shoulders, the curling brown hair on his chest. The pictures had played through her mind ever since the night he'd almost made love to her.

When Allison arrived with Jase at the school cafeteria an hour later, most of the chairs were taken. The cafeteria tables had been folded and rolled against the walls. About one hundred folding chairs were set up, facing two tables that were pushed together to make one long one. Council members were already seated up there. She spotted Chuck and Rita on the front right side of the cafeteria.

Jase murmured to her, close enough that his breath brushed her ear, "I have to sit up front."

Allison just nodded. Seeing Gloria over on the left, she crossed to her and took the empty seat beside her.

She watched as the men up front greeted Jase. She could see he was liked and respected. Dressed in his sheriff's uniform, he looked very official among the men with shirts and ties. Before he sat down, he took off his hat and set it on the counter behind them.

At exactly seven o'clock, the mayor called the meeting to order. He held a portable microphone that he could pass from member to member if necessary. He was short, with gray, thinning hair and glasses, yet when he spoke, the room became quiet. His voice carried a note of authority everyone seemed to respect.

Several of the council members had reports to make. After each, there were questions from the general public. The longest discussion centered around the proposal for a new discount store to come into Red Bluff. Some of the small businessmen were opposed because it would hurt their businesses, but residents liked the idea of the convenience. It wasn't a question that was going to be settled at this meeting. After the mayor decided to conclude the discussion for now, he handed the microphone to Jase.

Jase glanced down at the paper in front of him, raised his head and smiled at everyone. She could tell he was comfortable talking to the group.

After he told them their tax money was going to be used to replace the stoplight that was in need of repair on Rio and Third streets, he announced that a schedule would be posted for the painting of new crosswalks before September.

Suddenly a woman about ten rows back on the right waved her hand at him.

With a smile that said he didn't mind being interrupted, he acknowledged her. "Yes, Lorraine. You have a question about the crosswalks?"

"I don't have a question about the crosswalks, but I have another one."

The woman Jase had called by name looked to be in her sixties. Her brown hair was streaked with gray and caught at her neck in a bun held tight in a net. Allison couldn't help but wonder if Jase knew most of the citizens by name, or if the same ones always turned up for the town council meetings and became familiar to him.

"Go ahead," he said with a nod.

"Since you're sheriff and all, and therefore a role model in this community, I want to know how long you're going to have that woman living with you?"

A hush fell over the cafeteria, and Allison felt as if the breath had been knocked from her. Chuck and Rita glanced at her.

Gloria patted her hand. "Don't you mind her. She lives back in the Dark Ages."

Jase's expression, friendly before, became cold, hard and set. "I don't think that fits into the realm of community business, Lorraine."

"Well, I sure think it does," she argued. "You have a position in this community, and I just don't think it's proper. Elections are coming up and I think we all deserve an explanation."

Allison's heart was racing so fast she could hardly

catch her breath. She'd never meant to hurt Jase's reputation. He needed a good one in order to get re-elected. If her visit here cost him the job he loved…

There was only one thing she could do.

Standing, she hurried out of the cafeteria. She didn't want to be pointed out to the whole community. She didn't want Jase to have to defend her in public.

She'd just closed the door behind her and was walking down the hall when Gloria came hurrying after her. "Allison. Didn't you come with Jase?"

The urge to flee had been so strong she hadn't even thought about that. "Yes, I did. But I can walk. It's not that far."

"Don't be silly. I don't need to stay for the rest of this meeting. I'll drive you home."

Home. It was funny, but she'd almost starting thinking of Jase's house as that.

"I want you to know something." Gloria's tone was troubled. "People think I'm an old busybody, but I didn't tell anyone about you staying there with Jase."

Allison tried to give Gloria a reassuring smile. "I believe you. Lots of people knew I was staying with him. I should have foreseen this happening."

"I'm sure Jase will set them all straight."

"I don't want him to have to set them straight. I'm going to pack up and find a motel in Albuquerque."

Gloria shook her head as they walked down the hall. "I don't think he'll like that."

"That will be the best thing for him and probably for me, too."

Less than fifteen minutes later, Allison was in Jase's guest bedroom packing her suitcase. When

Gloria had dropped her off at the driveway, the older woman had seen Allison's determination, but she'd said, "Think about this before you leave. I hope you change your mind."

Allison had patted Gloria's hand. "Thanks for bringing me back. I'll give you a call and let you know where I'm staying. Maybe we can visit again before I fly back to Richmond."

Now tears came to her eyes, and she blinked them away. She was becoming fond of Gloria.

She was quickly slipping her makeup into her cosmetics bag when she heard the front door open. Resolutely she zippered the bag and laid it in her suitcase.

Suddenly Jase McGraw filled the doorway. "Why in the hell did you run out like that?" His expression was thunderous, his voice angry.

She moved to the dresser and picked up a bottle of perfume that wouldn't fit into her cosmetic bag. "I left because it was the best thing for you. I'm going to drive into Albuquerque and get a motel room."

"The hell you are. We're not doing anything wrong. There was no reason for you to run out as if we were."

She wouldn't meet his gaze. "No, we're not doing anything wrong. But do you want to lose your job?"

He came over and took her by the shoulders. "Some things are more important than my job. Like friendship."

She twisted away from him and kept on packing the belongings she'd scattered on the bed.

"Allison…"

"It's best if I leave, Jase. You know it and I know it."

Then suddenly, she felt his hand on her shoulder

again and she was in his arms, his mouth demanding and possessive on hers. She got lost for a moment in everything Jase was. The earth whirled with the brush of his lips and the touch of his tongue and the strength of his arms.

But then she wrenched away. "Don't! Just let me go. Even if you wanted more than one night of…whatever this is between us, I don't know if I can ever trust a man again!"

Jase wasn't sure what he'd expected to do when he'd taken Allison into his arms. Convince her to stay by kissing her senseless? Convince her to stay by having sex with her? Convince her to stay somehow with the right kiss, the right touch, maybe even the right words?

But now, shocked at her admission, he dropped his hands and stared at her. "What do you mean you'll never trust a man again?"

This time when she turned away from him and didn't answer, he didn't touch her. Instead he demanded forcefully, "Allison, tell me what you meant."

Maybe it was the commanding tone of his voice, maybe it was the feeling underneath, but something nudged her slowly around to face him again. She looked stricken, as if someone had just died, and he wished he could take the pain from her eyes. But he couldn't. All he could do was wait until she told him what was beneath it all.

"I didn't want you to know," she said in a whisper.

"Know what?"

"Dave was having an affair when he died."

One after another, questions clicked through Jase's mind. "How do you know?"

"I found letters from Tanya—his partner—to him. They were explicit letters. Not only about what was going on between them, but filled with dates and times. I thought back to those dates and times—his late hours, his excuses." She shook her head. "Other people had to know about it and I was the *last* one to know. Do you know how humiliated I was? Do you know how stupid I feel?"

"You didn't suspect?" Jase asked, still trying to absorb it.

"That's the question probably everyone's asking, including me. How could I not know? How could I believe all his excuses? How could I believe his work had him so stressed out that sex didn't matter to him as much anymore? But nothing stood out!" She rushed on. "Not his working late, or the new styles of clothes he bought, or the charges on our credit card I knew nothing about. They were sporadic. I thought he bought something he needed and didn't tell me about."

Then her voice cracked, and tears ran down her cheeks and Jase didn't know what to do to help her. She was still suffering through it, questioning everything.

He thought about the night when Dave ran away from the consequences of hot-wiring the car. Had that been a sign of the kind of man he'd turn out to be? "Allison, none of this was your fault."

"Of course it was," she cried. "It was *all* my fault. What am I lacking? What did I do wrong as a wife? Why couldn't he keep his vows to me?"

This was the deep pain he'd glimpsed in her eyes.

It wasn't only grief that had worked her over this past year, it had been Dave's betrayal. He couldn't keep from enfolding her into his arms then and holding her while she cried. "Let it out," he murmured. "Let it all out."

Allison's tears and then her sobs shuddered through her body and Jase just held on to her, trying to tell her she was safe. As her tears wet his shirt, he stroked her hair, whispering to her, assuring her there was nothing wrong with her, that she wasn't the one at fault, that she couldn't blame herself.

But when she finally leaned away from him and looked into his eyes, he knew she *did* blame herself. Turning away, she murmured, "I'm sorry. I never meant to break down like that."

This time he wasn't going to let her run or evade him. Taking her hand, he pulled her over to the bed and tugged her down beside him. "Breaking down isn't always a bad thing. Have you talked to anyone else about this?"

"No!"

"Not even your parents?"

"*Especially* not my parents. I don't want their pity. I don't want them to know I couldn't keep my marriage together."

"Allison..."

"It's true, Jase. What kind of judgment do I have? Was I so self-absorbed and so complacent with my marriage that I didn't see any warning signals? If I'd have known there were problems, we could have gone to counseling. If I had only known..." Her breath caught and he slipped his arm around her. Finally she laid her head on his shoulder.

He meant the embrace to be friendly. He meant it

to be comforting. But his jaw was brushing her hair. With each breath, he inhaled her scent, and the softness of her skin under his fingertips made him want to touch her in anything but friendly ways.

Then she murmured, "I've got to leave, Jase. I don't want to put your job in jeopardy."

"Do you think I'm going to let you leave after what you just told me?"

"I've been living with it for a year," she said against his chest. "It's not going to go away."

"No, it's not. But you've got to come to terms with it or you won't be able to go on with your life. As far as my job goes, it's not in any jeopardy. Lorraine is the town puritan and as I told her and everyone else, you and I are friends, and my friendship with you is more important than public opinion."

She leaned away from his embrace then and looked up at him. "You said that?"

"I sure did. Even got a round of applause for it. Maria is going to be upset about all of it though, because I left before I got a chance to remind the folks about checking over their kids' immunization records before school starts, let alone announcing the clinic's hours will be changing in August."

Now that he'd brought up the subject of Maria again, purposely in part to see how Allison would react, he sensed her withdrawal. So he went on, "I stopped at the clinic yesterday to get Maria's notes on what she wanted me to discuss since she couldn't be there tonight."

Allison's shiny green eyes met his. "That's why you were there?"

"That, and because I hadn't talked to her for a

while. I took some sandwiches over and we had lunch.''

She looked away again. ''I see.''

''I don't know if you *do* see, Allison. You acted kind of funny when you saw me there yesterday. What are you thinking?''

After long moments of silence, she finally answered him. ''I'm wondering if you don't feel more for Maria than you say you do. I'm wondering if you're denying it because she's still married.''

He'd gone down that road with himself before. He liked Maria and he could talk to her about almost anything, but there was no zing there, not like there was with Allison.

''I told you before,'' he said gruffly, ''we're friends.''

''And you told everyone there tonight that you and I are friends.''

She'd corralled him on that one. He raked his hand through his hair. ''Look, you and I...the truth is—I've always wanted you. But I kept away because of Dave. Now I should probably still stay away from you because of Dave. You've got a lot to sort out. And I think I have a good way for you to do it.''

She looked as if she was trying to take in what he'd said. But then she asked, ''What would be a good way to sort it out?''

''How would you like to go camping? We'll get away from everyone, trek into the Gila Wilderness, and spend a couple of nights out under the stars. I think it might be good for both of us.''

''Can you get away now?''

''A few days won't be a problem. What do you think?''

"I don't know. Are you sure I can do it?"

He couldn't help but smile. "I think you can do anything you set your mind to."

But she still didn't look sure. "You're positive your job's not in jeopardy if I stay?"

"I'm positive. The truth is, if it is, then I don't want to be sheriff here."

"But you like Red Bluff."

"I do, but I suppose I could find another place to like just as well." He'd always tried not to get attached to anyone or anything. Life was simpler that way.

Her gaze searched his face and then her doubts seemed to vanish. "All right. When do you want to leave?"

"I'll clear off my desk tomorrow and we'll leave early Thursday morning. In the meantime..." He paused. "Think about what happened with Dave if you have to. But don't let it weigh you down so much that you forget that he's gone and you're still here."

He wanted even more for her than that. He wanted even more for himself. But she wasn't ready to trust, and he wasn't ready to make any promises he might not be able to keep.

It was five o'clock when Allison and Jase left his house on Thursday morning. He'd told her they'd have about a two-hour drive to the wilderness area. They hadn't talked much since Tuesday night after the town council meeting. At first, Allison had felt as if a burden had fallen from her shoulders once Jase knew. But on the other hand, Dave's betrayal—Jase's best friend's betrayal—stood like another wall between them. Yesterday had been filled with prepara-

tions for this trip, though Jase had already had many
of the supplies they needed since he'd trekked into
the back country of the Gila Wilderness before.

At first enthusiastic about the trip, she was now
becoming apprehensive as they stopped at a ranger
station. What if she couldn't keep up with Jase? What
if she wasn't fit enough for this kind of hike? What
if he saw she wasn't an independent woman after all,
but a scaredy-cat who'd been too cautious all her life
and was now afraid of new experiences?

And what if he never kissed or touched her again
because of what she'd said about not being able to
trust a man? What if he thought Dave's death and
betrayal had left too great a wound to ever heal?

She didn't have any of the answers. She just knew
that what she felt with Jase was nothing like she'd
ever felt before.

"We'll be there soon," Jase finally said as he
drove down another side road. "July and August is a
busy time for hikers. That's why I like the back country. On the trails I've used before, I haven't run into
many folks."

"And that's good?"

"It's what I want when I come out here. But you'll
see for yourself. If you want to do the tourist thing
and visit the cliff dwellings, we can do that before we
go home."

All alone in the wilderness with Jase McGraw. It
was an exciting yet terrifying thought.

Off the paved road, Jase took a series of twists and
turns and finally parked in a clearing. Theirs was the
only vehicle there, though she could see tire tracks in
the packed earth.

Jase unloaded their gear.

"How big is all this?" she asked.

"The Gila Wilderness takes up over half a million acres, more than a thousand square miles."

"You're kidding."

"Nope."

When they'd stopped at the ranger station, Jase had given the man a duplicate copy of the trail they were going to take. Now she could see why. A person could get lost and never be found.

The last thing Jase took from the car was the map. When he opened it, it was about three feet square. Now he poked his finger at it and her gaze followed. "This is where we're going." He wiggled the map. "This is what we use to get there. It has everything on it including the springs and creeks. I double-checked water sources with the ranger. I also got suggestions on the best places to cross the river. There aren't any footbridges."

"So we're going to get wet?" she asked lightly.

He laughed. "Maybe. But it's been pretty dry. We shouldn't have any trouble." With a wink he added, "That's why you brought an extra pair of socks. Just in case the ones you're wearing get wet."

She smiled at him weakly. He'd told her exactly what to pack to keep her backpack light yet comprehensively useful.

Allison told herself to relax and get into the spirit of the trek. "What kind of trees are these?" she asked, looking around. Many looked like pine, but she couldn't tell for sure.

"Emory oaks, junipers. This morning we'll be in the drier zone. You'll learn how to look and listen and see things you wouldn't see anywhere else. We're going to be climbing, so make sure you tell me if you need to rest and drink. The temperature will probably go into the nineties. Are you ready?''

"As ready as I'll ever be," she murmured.

Grinning at her, he helped her with her backpack.

They didn't talk at first as they hiked. Allison tried to get used to everything around her, and as the minutes swept by, she forgot about time, she forgot about Richmond and Red Bluff, and she tried to take in a land that seemed absolutely unspoiled, without humans—or at least lots of humans—trampling across it. When she caught sight of her first prairie dog, she grabbed Jase's arm and he just laughed. She recognized the sagebrush, but after that, he pointed out the creosote and yucca and scrub brush. The ponderosa pines were amazing and she soon forgot that her hiking boots were new, that she'd been scared early that morning, that she'd have to return to her life eventually.

They were so engrossed in the hike, it was late by the time they stopped for lunch. She had no idea how far they'd come and didn't really care. She felt as if she were in the midst of an entirely new world, and she liked it.

The sun was high and hot as they settled for lunch near a creek bed that was almost dry. They sat under the shade of a few cottonwoods as they lunched on beef jerky, PowerBars and trail mix.

After Jase took a few slugs of water, he wiped the back of his hand across his mouth and studied Allison. "So what do you think about backpacking?"

"I'm glad my backpack isn't as heavy as yours," she teased. But then she looked at the scenery around her. "I can see why you like it and come out here when you want to get away from everything."

"When I come here on my own, I realize why it was Geronimo's refuge. Frank's the one who first told me about this trail. He comes here backpacking, too. Oh, by the way," Jase continued, "when I stopped out there to check how he was doing last night, he told me to tell you, if you meet any creatures out here, they'll be friendlier than Lorraine was."

"Any repercussions at the sheriff's office yesterday?" she asked, wishing she could be as casual about what had happened as Jase. They hadn't talked about it again...or about Dave.

"Only folks stopping in to tell me what I did was my own business and that I was right about friendship being more important than public opinion. Forget about it, Allison. I have."

But she couldn't forget about it, nor what had come afterward. From the look in his eyes, she could tell he hadn't, either.

He leaned an elbow on a stack of rocks beside him. "What kind of marriage did you and Dave have?"

On one hand, she felt uncomfortable talking with Jase about her marriage, yet on the other she knew she could tell him just about anything. "I'm not sure now," she responded. "We were high school sweethearts getting married, planning a life together. I thought it was a good one, yet..."

"Yet what?" Jase asked gently.

"My mom and dad seem to have something more."

"Something more?"

"I don't know how to explain it. Dave and I...well, it was like we knew we were right for each other, and everybody *else* thought we were right for each other. But my mom and dad seem to have something...deep.

Dave and I always seemed to be walking on the surface.'' She shook her head. "And now I wonder what we had at all.''

"Dave wronged you, Allison. You're never going to really know why, and you're going to be torturing yourself if you keep asking the question. From what I've seen, most marriages don't work. My sister's an exception. Maybe your parents are, too. But they're the lucky ones, the unusual ones.''

"You don't think marriage can be an absolute melding of hearts and souls?''

"I think that's right up there with believing in Santa Claus,'' Jase answered wryly.

"But isn't it important to believe?'' Allison asked, more serious than she'd ever been.

"Believing is one thing. Expecting too much is another.''

He finished his beef jerky. "We'll be getting into higher country soon, and we can keep going till sundown. Is that okay with you?''

It would be a relief to be hiking again instead of talking about all this. It would be a relief to be less conscious of Jase's gaze on her, of her feelings for him, of her yearning to be held in his arms. "Sounds good to me. I'm ready when you are.''

Sitting up, he saw the cellophane that had wrapped the beef jerky. It had drifted into a crevice between two rocks. He reached for it, then swore and jerked his hand away.

"What is it?''

Quickly shoving the rock aside, he spotted what he was looking for. "A scorpion stung me.''

Allison thought about all the hiking they'd done

today, how far they'd come. She thought about the little she knew about scorpion stings.

Then she panicked.

Chapter Nine

"Scorpion stings can be dangerous," Allison said as her hands shook and she went to Jase.

"This one's not dangerous. I saw him. There aren't that many lethal ones. This'll just be uncomfortable."

Already his hand was swelling and Allison threw off her panic, naturally drawing on her nursing skills. "Let's put a cool cloth on it, then we'll head back."

"We're *not* heading back."

"Jase! It's the only logical thing to do."

"We're not heading back. I'll be fine."

"I think we should turn around," she maintained.

There was a full minute of silence. Jase finally broke it. "If we turn around, it won't be because of this sting. Maybe you didn't really want to come out here at all. If you don't like it…if you're bored, or too hot…"

She could lie to him. She could say she was bored and too hot, and he'd probably turn around. But she couldn't do that with Jase. "I do like it out here. I've never been anywhere like this before."

He attempted a smile. "Then let's go on. We'll be heading into cooler territory soon, and I know I'll be okay."

In that moment, she realized exactly how much she loved Jase McGraw. If anything happened to him... "If we go on, I'm going to watch you like a hawk."

His smile widened. "That's not exactly a *bad* thing."

Shaking her head, she took a washcloth out of her backpack. She had no idea what to do for a scorpion sting, and if Jase wouldn't let her treat him, her only recourse was to watch him very carefully.

"Let me take your pulse," she commanded.

"You're serious about this, aren't you?" he asked with a sigh.

"Absolutely. I won't keep going unless you let me take care of you."

With a wry grimace, he presented his wrist to her. "Go ahead. Take it."

She did, and found that it was running a little fast. But that in itself didn't mean a whole lot. Especially when she looked up into his dark brown eyes and found the fire there. Her pulse was running faster, too.

They packed up their gear and had hiked about an hour when she noticed that Jase was slowing down. When she looked at him, she asked, "Are you all right?"

"If I tell you the truth, you have to promise me not to panic. I know the symptoms for this, and they're uncomfortable, not life-threatening."

"What's going on, Jase?"

"I'm a little queasy, and my hand hurts. Period. Now, come on."

"Not until I check you again."

In spite of his scowl, she took his pulse and checked his breathing. He seemed all right, but she wasn't taking any chances. Every twenty minutes or so, in spite of his protests, she monitored him carefully.

When they stopped for supper, Allison could tell Jase's hand was bothering him more, because he was hardly moving it.

"I have acetaminophen if it'll help the pain," she offered.

"After we're set up and get supper going."

Supper consisted of dried beans and rice that they cooked over a small fire, and two candy bars for dessert. After the exertion, Allison had found herself very hungry. But as she watched Jase move the food around his plate, she suspected he was hurting—a lot. Going to her backpack, she took out the acetaminophen and gave them to him. He took the pills without a word.

As they leaned against large rocks, watching the campfire dwindle, Jase said, "Distract me."

"How?" She could think of ways he probably wouldn't want to consider right now.

With one of his half smiles, he answered, "Tell me why you became a nurse."

Glad to do anything to help him, she explained, "When I was ten, I had a friend who was diagnosed with cancer. Mary fought it for five years, but she died just before her fifteenth birthday." Allison paused for a few moments, remembering. Then she added, "I watched the nurses care for her. They really helped make her days brighter. I decided I wanted to do that for others.''

After a pause, when she noticed he'd closed his eyes, she went on, ''I'd like to become a nurse practitioner. That way, I could do more.''

Jase's legs were stretched out in front of him, his head pillowed against the rock. After a while he opened his eyes and glanced at the fire, now almost out. ''I think I'd like to turn in. We only got a few hours of sleep last night.''

Jase seemed to need a lot less sleep than she did. She suspected he was simply too uncomfortable sitting here and didn't want her watching him.

His swollen hand looked worse than before, yet when she took his pulse again, it was regular and steady, and his respiration was normal. It seemed that the scorpion sting wasn't any worse than a bee sting. But bee stings could be tremendously painful, and she suspected this was no different.

Jase unrolled his bedroll one-handed, and she knew if she offered to help he'd refuse.

Taking the bull by his horns, so to speak, Allison arranged her bedroll right next to Jase's. He quirked an eyebrow.

''I want to monitor your breathing. I want to make sure you're okay.''

''And if I say that's not necessary?''

''I'll tell you to drop the macho act and be reasonable.''

Straightening, he faced her toe-to-toe. ''It's not an act, Allison. Yes, the hand hurts. But I'd just as soon go crawl in a hole by myself.''

She'd guessed he didn't want her to see him hurting. "That's exactly why I'm not going to let you," she declared sweetly.

He pinned her with a hard stare. "I have to take care of some elementary essentials before I turn in. Do you want to hold my hand while I do that, too?"

If he meant to unnerve her, she wasn't going to let him. "Nope. I'll take care of my essentials and meet you back here. Do I need to watch out for bears?"

As he disappeared beyond a few ponderosa pines, he called back, "No. Just nurses who won't let their patients rest in peace."

Finally they settled side by side, stretched out beneath the stars. But Jase was restless, and she wanted to do something to help him. After he rolled onto his side, his back to her, she rested her hand on his shoulder, and then started making large circles on his back.

"Allison..."

"Shh," she murmured. "This will help." She kept up a soothing rhythm, not massaging, just gently comforting...rubbing...taking his attention from his hand onto something a little more pleasurable. Eventually she could feel him relaxing under her fingers. When his breathing became even and deep, she knew he was asleep, and she could rest, too.

Sometime in the middle of the night, Jase shifted onto his back. He murmured to her, "Come here."

Without hesitating, she lay in the crook of his shoulder, her arm across his chest, holding him. With his chin resting on the top of her head, they both fell asleep again until morning.

When Jase awakened, he realized he felt better. His hand still hurt some, but it wasn't the throbbing, aching pain of yesterday. He knew he'd scared Allison. But he hadn't wanted to turn back. He'd wanted this time with her out under the stars. Only it had turned out much differently than he'd expected. Yet something about holding her throughout the night had been as satisfying as anything else that might have happened. It brought a satisfaction he hadn't experienced before. He didn't want to let her out of his embrace, but he knew that he had to. He knew she wasn't ready for anything else.

How could he teach her to trust him? Did he really want to try?

He'd never imagined he could be faithful to one woman—or *want* to be faithful to one woman. But Allison's presence in his life had changed that. Was willpower enough? Was his own sense of honor enough to keep him faithful? Could he shake his own history, as well as the example his father had set? He didn't know. But he did know he had to find the answers before he even tried to make a move on Allison, before the bond between them grew stronger than it already was. With her nestled close to him, her soft body molded against his, the last thing he wanted to do was move away from her. Yet he had to.

If he'd thought he could extricate himself easily, he'd been mistaken. She opened her eyes as soon as he shifted his weight.

"How do you feel?" she murmured, her hand still resting over the beat of his heart.

"Better."

She looked relieved as her gaze searched his face. He suspected her examination was clinical as much as anything else.

"You had me worried yesterday," she said.

Trying at a lightness he didn't feel, he did move

away from her then and sat up, joking, "Afraid you'd have to carry me out of here?"

"No. Afraid you were a lot worse than you were letting on, and I'd be powerless to help you."

She looked so unbelievably pretty, propped on her elbow on her side, her hair mussed, her eyes still a bit hazy from sleep. Another woman faced with her situation yesterday might have gone into hysterics. Allison Rhodes was one gutsy lady...and more. He remembered how badly his hand had hurt last night. How nauseous he'd felt. How unbelievably calming, yet distracting, her hand had been on his back. "Thanks for what you did last night."

"I didn't do anything."

"You helped me relax so I could fall asleep."

She sat up and brushed her hair behind her ear. "I just wanted to take your pain away. I think there's a healing power in touch."

How right she was about that. He wanted to take *her* pain away, too, but he was afraid his touch might make it worse. He'd never felt the sting of betrayal, because he'd never gotten close enough to anyone to give them the chance to betray him. But Allison had given everything she was to her husband and her marriage. Jase felt angry for her, and with her. Yet behind the anger, he could see in her eyes a world of hurt that might never heal.

Before he took her in his arms again, he climbed to his feet and took a deep, bracing breath of morning air. It had dropped into the sixties last night, but he hadn't even noticed with Allison curled beside him. "We can take our time hiking this morning, then we'll start the loop back. We should reach the truck by early afternoon tomorrow. So if you want to stop at the cliff dwellings, we can.''

''I'd like that. I might not have a chance to see them again.''

Right. She'd be going back to Richmond soon. And he'd damn well better remember it.

Allison heard Jase's SUV on Sunday around noon. She knew the sound of its engine. She even remembered the license plate—the numbers were consecutive. But she heard another vehicle stopping, too. Looking out the window, she saw a green sedan.

Since Jase had taken off work for three days, he'd gone in today, telling her he'd probably be staying late into the evening. Already their trip seemed like something suspended in time—an extraordinary experience that wasn't real. She'd spent that one night in Jase's arms and loved it. She'd felt safe and treasured. But the next morning he'd put distance between them again and kept it there.

Because he was trying to protect her? Because she didn't know if she could ever have a trusting relationship with a man again? Because *he* didn't want to get more deeply involved?

As they'd hiked through oaks and sycamores and pines, as they'd spotted a fox and even an eagle, she'd thought about everything that had happened over the past year—and throughout her marriage. She still felt as if she'd *done* something wrong, as if somehow *she* was to blame for Dave looking elsewhere.

When she and Jase had stopped the second night, they'd spread their bedrolls side by side. She'd longed to be held in his arms again, but they hadn't touched.

They hadn't talked much, either, and she'd felt the gap between them growing wider.

So she was surprised to see him coming home now, until she recognized the couple getting out of the sedan. It was George and Cecelia Natchez, and George was carrying Pablo in his arms.

Allison swung open the door enthusiastically, noticing Cecelia was carrying a package gaily wrapped in red. Then she gave the young mother a careful hug because of her rib. After she shook hands with George, she tickled Pablo under the chin. "I'm so happy to see you. What brings you back to Red Bluff?"

Jase stood silently behind them.

"We came back to thank you properly," Cecelia answered. "We're leaving for California in a few weeks. George is taking a new job out there. I wanted to give you something to remember us by, to show you how much we appreciate how you helped us."

Jase opened a six-inch square box he was carrying so Allison could see what was inside. "It's a hand-tooled belt," he explained.

She ran her fingers over the workmanship. "It's beautiful."

Cecelia presented her with an oddly shaped present. "I hope you like this."

Allison motioned them into the living room. She'd picked up the bedroll after Jase had left this morning and straightened up. Now when she went to sit on the sofa, Cecelia followed her and sat beside her while George stood jiggling Pablo.

Allison couldn't keep her gaze from the baby. "I've missed him. You've got a wonderful little boy there."

George smiled. "And we know it."

Turning her attention to the package, she carefully tore off the paper, revealing a basket. But it wasn't just a simple basket. There were figures, as well as symbols, woven onto the side. Allison examined and appreciated the handwork. "This is beautiful."

"I'm Apache," Cecelia said. "My grandmother taught me how to make this."

"You wove this yourself?"

"I've been doing it since I was a little girl. But I made this one for you because this is a special basket."

"Special?"

Cecelia smiled. "It's called a harmony basket. It's made of willow and sedge, and my grandmother showed me how to use wildflowers for dye."

Allison examined the beads and feathers on it.

"Every basket tells a story," Cecelia explained.

"What story does this one tell?" Allison asked curiously.

After glancing shyly at Jase and George, Cecelia said softly to Allison, "It tells the story of a man and a woman—their separate lives becoming one."

Allison felt her heart beat faster as she looked up at Jase. But he wasn't looking back. He'd taken Pablo from George and was holding him up in the air. "I think you've grown two inches," he said to the little boy.

Pablo waved his arms and grinned, showing a new tooth.

"Thank you so much for the basket," Allison said to Cecelia, a bit embarrassed, knowing what Cecelia was implying by giving it to her. Then she set it on the coffee table and went over to Jase. "Can I hold him for a little while?"

Jase handed over the baby with the comment, "I wondered how long it would take you."

Allison invited George and Cecelia to stay for the afternoon and for supper, but they insisted that they couldn't. They were on the way to Cecelia's aunt's for one last visit before they left for California. After tall glasses of lemonade and an hour of conversation, George said they should be going. He took Pablo from Allison's lap where she had been holding him most of the time, and went outside with Jase, leaving the women to say goodbye.

"I didn't mean to embarrass you by telling you the story of the basket," Cecelia said. "But I can feel the connection between you and the sheriff. And the basket's just a reminder that harmony will come, if you let it."

Allison smiled. "I sure could use some harmony in my life."

Cecelia looked as if she debated with herself for a moment, but then said, "If you put something of yours in the basket, along with something of Sheriff McGraw's, you might find the harmony coming a little sooner."

Allison didn't scoff at any tradition. What Cecelia was suggesting was like a wish or a prayer, or, in New Age terms, sort of creating an image of what she wanted to happen. "I'll remember that," she told Cecelia, giving the young mother a hug, glad she'd had the opportunity to meet her and get to know her a little better.

After George and Cecelia had left, and Jase had gone back to the office, Allison stared at the small basket on the coffee table and suddenly had the desire to wish and imagine…to pray and to dream. Today she'd worn the barrette Jase had given her. She unfastened it and dropped it into the basket. Now she needed something of Jase's. Not wanting to invade his privacy but needing something personal, she stepped into his bedroom and looked around. She hadn't come into this room often, just to put clean laundry on his bed mostly.

Going over to the dresser, she stood there, examining everything on its top. There was a change dish with a few coins in it and a bottle of cologne. Then she saw what she was looking for. It was the bolo tie that went with his uniform. Only this one must be a spare since he was wearing one today. Lifting it, she looked at the New Mexico emblem and the black string, only hesitating for a moment before she took it into the living room and slipped it into the basket with her barrette. If he asked her where it was, she'd tell him. She might even tell him why she'd put it there!

Then she closed her eyes and said a prayer, made a wish, and tried to believe in a dream.

The sun was sinking below the horizon when Jase came home. He'd stopped at Frank's to check on him, and the man was doing fine. It had been a stop to postpone the inevitable…to postpone coming home to Allison and facing all the turmoil he felt about her. He'd thought about procrastinating even further by stopping at the Cantina, too. But that wouldn't ease the ache in his heart and his body that had begun at his niece's christening and had intensified this afternoon as Allison had held Pablo. The picture of Allison pregnant with his child had been gnawing at him all day, intensifying everything else he was dealing with between the two of them—his feelings, their attraction to each other, her eventual return to Richmond.

On top of all of it, a question kept leaping at him. What would she say if he asked her to stay?

The house was quiet, and he found her sitting on the patio, gazing into the streaking colors of the end of day. She looked so beautiful, bathed in the sunset lights, it was hard for him to swallow.

When he opened the glass door and stepped outside, she glanced at him over her shoulder. "Hi."

"Hi."

"I guess you had mounds of work to handle after being gone."

"Enough." He took off his hat and set it beside the chair. But he didn't sit down. He was too restless over the question he couldn't get out of his mind.

She stood, then, saying, "I had supper with Gloria, and she sent some chili over for you. I can heat it up."

He caught her arm as she turned to go into the house. "No."

Looking up at him, puzzled, she asked, "You've already eaten?"

"No."

Her gaze locked to his then. "What's the matter?"

"Nothing. I—" Taking her by the shoulders now, he decided he might as well stop torturing himself. Better to know than to wonder. "Would you consider staying in Red Bluff?"

Her eyes became wide. "With you?"

He hadn't thought that far. "Maybe. I don't know."

With her voice quivering slightly, she asked, "Why?"

Everything seemed jumbled in his head. His father's history with women. His mother's heartache. His own past. The need for Allison he couldn't shake. Like an avalanche falling on him, he was tired of dealing with all of it, and he felt too vulnerable trying to lay his feelings on the line.

He blurted out, "Because I want to take you to bed. Because I want to lie between your legs and hold you, and lose myself in you and make you lose yourself in me." There was more he wanted, so much more, but he couldn't get a grasp on it yet...couldn't jump headlong into something so foreign to everything he'd known.

She was looking at him as if the words had painted pictures for her, too...as if she wanted the same thing.

Then he was kissing her, and she was kissing him, and the colors of the sunset seemed to surround them. Her fingers slid into his hair, her tongue mated with his, her body melted into him. But then in contrast to her first response, her body stiffened, and she pushed away.

Her eyes were shiny with tears. "I don't know if I'm ready for this. I don't know if I can change my entire life for an...for an affair."

"Is your life so good in Richmond?" he asked in almost a growl, angry because she couldn't give him an unqualified yes.

"Maybe I haven't given it a chance to be good."

Richmond or Red Bluff. A future coming from a past she'd known or a different one with him. "What

you're saying is that you can't take a chance on *me*.
I know we're different, Allison. I know you're used
to green grass and refined friends and food that
doesn't burn when it hits your stomach. But I also
thought that you might have the courage to reach for
something different.''

"It's more than that, Jase. My family's in Richmond, my job, everyone I know."

She was making excuses, and they both knew it.
Maybe she was still in love with Dave in spite of what
he'd done to her. Maybe what she felt for Jase wasn't
nearly what he felt for her. He snatched up his hat,
set it on his head and opened the sliding glass door.
"I'm going to the Cantina for a while."

"Do you want me to leave?" she asked in a low
voice that trembled.

"Maybe that *would* be best. Maybe it's time we
both took hold of our own lives again."

As he strode through the living room and out the
front door, he swore. He hadn't meant to be that
abrupt. He hadn't meant to be that hard. She was
trying to get over what Dave had done to her. But
throughout his life, his poverty and his background
had made him feel like a second-class citizen. Even
all of those years on the Richmond Police Force, he'd
felt as if everyone had known his background and had
congratulated him for overcoming it. But he'd .ever
felt equal. Not to Dave. Not to Clark Rhodes. Especially not to Allison.

Out here, he'd found a life where no one looked at
where he'd been, only at who he was. Apparently
Allison wasn't willing to give who he was a chance.

Before Jase went to the Cantina, he drove around
for a while. He opened all the windows in the SUV

and went out on a dark, lonely stretch of road, going over the speed limit and not caring, letting his mind go blank in the rush of air and speed. But he didn't do it for very long, because he remembered he was the sheriff of Red Bluff. He had to set an example. He had to believe in the laws he helped enforce. Easing his boot off the accelerator, he turned around and headed back toward Red Bluff, toward the Cantina, where some tamales might help fill up the emptiness inside of him.

On a Sunday night, the restaurant was busy. He asked for a table on the patio, knowing it would be quieter out there. But when the waitress led him there, he saw Maria sitting alone at a round table in the darkest corner, a sheaf of papers in her hand.

When she looked up, she looked terribly upset, and Jase said to the waitress, "I won't be needing a table of my own. I'll be joining her. And I won't be ready to order for a while."

He could tell Maria had been crying. "What's wrong?" he asked, sitting down, glad to have something else to think about besides Allison.

"Tony is suing me for a divorce." Her tears began falling again.

Jase moved his chair closer to her. "What are you going to do?"

"I don't know. I was so angry when he left. But I've missed him so much while he's been gone. I thought when he got back, somehow we'd work everything out. But he's not coming back. At least not for another year. He sent a letter with the papers." Her voice broke.

"What else did he say?"

She stared down at the papers on the table as if she

couldn't believe what she'd read. "He said we can't have a marriage living thousands of miles apart. He says that if we end this now, we'll both be free to do whatever we want!"

"What do you want?" Jase asked gently.

"I *don't* want a divorce. But I don't want to leave my family, either."

"Why?"

She looked at Jase as if he were crazy. "Because...because...because I'm afraid," she ended softly.

"You're not afraid of anything."

She nodded. "Yes, I am, Jase. That's why I didn't go with him. I've always had my family around me, supporting me, cheering me on. I knew nothing about Africa, and suddenly Tony was jumping into going there, as if it was the greatest place on earth."

"It might be—if you were there with him." Jase knew Red Bluff would be the best place on earth if Allison stayed.

The song from the jukebox inside flowed onto the patio.

Eventually Maria went on. "In his letter, he said I didn't even try to understand, that I didn't even give Africa a chance. I guess he's right. I should have gone with him and at least seen what it was like. He describes the children there who need help, the people there who need help."

Maria had been terrifically unhappy for the past four months, though she'd tried to hide it most of the time. "You have a chance to be with the man you married and do the work you were trained for," Jase offered, sensing she needed a little push.

Looking up at him, she asked, "I've been a fool,

haven't I? Being stubborn all these months, refusing to see his side of it.''

"I don't know, have you?"

"Yes. Yes," she repeated more emphatically. "Either he doesn't love me anymore and he really wants this divorce, or he sent these papers to wake me up. Well, they've done that."

Her dark brown eyes were dry now, and Jase could see the determination growing in them. "What are you going to do?"

"I'm going to call Dr. Grover and tell him he has to come out of retirement until they can replace me at the clinic, and then I'm booking the first flight out tomorrow." Looking over at him, she asked, "Do you know what a good friend you are?"

He shook his head. "I didn't do anything."

"You listened and you asked the right questions. That was exactly what I needed." She threw her arms around him and gave him a huge hug.

Jase realized how much he'd miss Maria if she left. But he also realized that missing Maria would be entirely different from missing Allison. And as if he'd conjured her up, there Allison was, coming through the doorway from the restaurant to the patio. She saw him, and then she realized exactly what she was seeing. Maria was hugging him and he was hugging her. There was no doubt in Jase's mind what Allison was thinking. She didn't say a word, just turned, and hurried back through the restaurant.

He knew he had to go after her or regret it for the rest of his life.

Chapter Ten

Allison was halfway across the parking lot when Jase caught up to her and grasped her arm. "Don't run away like this. Let me tell you about—"

"I don't want to hear about it," she said, her eyes brimming with tears. She'd come here to tell Jase that maybe an affair was enough...that she wanted him to make love to her...that she wanted to explore all the feelings between them. She shook her head, unable to speak.

"You have to trust me, Allison. If you can't trust me, we don't even have friendship between us. Maria and I are friends. Her husband served her with divorce papers and she was upset."

"She'll be free now," Allison murmured, wondering if that mattered. Wondering if any man cared about vows and promises and planning a future for a lifetime.

"No, she won't be free. She's going to Africa to

join her husband, and I'm happy about that because she's my friend, and now she'll be happy, too."

Allison studied his face, every line and every crevice, and she knew he was telling the truth. But she also knew something else. What had happened just now, could happen again and again and again. "It doesn't matter."

"Of course it matters!" he exploded. "Don't you understand? There's nothing between me and Maria except some good, old-fashioned affection."

"You're the one who doesn't understand," she said in a low voice. "You want me to trust you. I just found out I can't. I just found out I can't trust *any* man. Every time I see you with another woman, I'll wonder. It's *me,* Jase, not you. I'm going back to your house and pack. I'm leaving for Virginia tomorrow morning."

"I am *not* Dave Rhodes," he said, his voice low and vehement.

"No, you're not. You could be the most honorable man in the world. But because of Dave, I don't know if I can believe that."

Under the parking lot light, Jase's face was stony. "Why are you letting him have this power over you? You're letting what he did control your life."

"Maybe I am, but I don't know what to do about it. It's not about Dave. This is about *me.* I couldn't keep him interested. I couldn't make him want to come home. I couldn't keep him in our bed." She couldn't stop the tears now. They were rolling down her cheeks, and she looked as if she'd lost everything.

Jase's thoughts and emotions churned as they stood there. He couldn't stand the idea of her going back to Virginia, and he obviously couldn't make her stay, either. Just as he was trying to get a handle on the best thing to say or do, his pager went off.

He swore, looked at the code on his readout, and knew he had to call in right away. "There's a burglary in progress, Allison. I've got to make this call now."

"It doesn't matter, Jase. I'm going back to your house to pack. Be careful, okay?"

He'd hardly nodded before she was running from him to her car.

It took him a few moments to remember he had work to do…to remind himself he was the sheriff of Red Bluff, and he was in charge of what might happen in the next half hour.

Jogging to his SUV, he snatched up his mobile phone. As he called in and listened to the dispatcher, he saw Allison's car leave the parking lot. There was a tightness in his chest that had begun when she'd run from the Cantina. Expelling a deep breath now to get rid of it, he listened to Clara's words, climbed into the SUV and headed for the main thoroughfare.

The call had come in from someone who had seen furtive activity in the house next door. The neighbor had known the occupants were away for the weekend. They'd called in a description and license number of a gray pickup truck, telling the dispatcher the direction the truck had taken.

When Jase had investigated the last robbery, he remembered a neighbor saying a gray truck had been seen cruising past the house a few days before. Now he told Clara to get an ID on the license and call for backup. Then he tossed the phone aside. Lights flashing, siren blaring, he sped up the main road. Virgil and Chuck were on patrol tonight, but they were on the other side of town. Rod and Wyatt were at the office, but Jase knew he could catch up to the pickup before they could. He lowered his foot on the accelerator, the burglars' license plate number burned into his mind.

At Jase's house, Allison heard the noise coming from the scanner as soon as she walked into the kitchen, but she tried to ignore it. Still, as she went into the bedroom, she couldn't. Jase was out there somewhere, chasing criminals.

After she pulled her suitcase and garment bag from the closet, she laid them on the bed and started throwing clothes inside. But the noise from the scanner buzzed in her ears. Leaving the suitcase opened, she returned to the kitchen and listened, telling herself she just wanted to make sure Jase was okay.

She was still shaking from their encounter in the parking lot. She was still shaking from thinking he'd gone to Maria for the physical satisfaction she wouldn't give him. She was still shaking because she seemed to have lost her ability to trust, and that scared her more than anything else.

Suddenly more calls on the scanner came through fast and furious, one right after the other. After listening to it for the past couple of weeks, she knew what some of the codes meant. There'd been an accident. An ambulance was heading to the scene. She heard the license plate number of Jase's vehicle being rattled off, along with another, and her heart practically stopped.

He'd been in an accident. No! Nothing could happen to Jase. She loved him too much.

The basket Cecelia had given her was sitting on the

coffee table in the living room. It still held her barrette and Jase's tie. If he'd noticed it, he hadn't said anything about it. If she'd expected some ritual to bring them together...

No ritual could do that, but *she* could.

She remembered the look in Jase's eyes when he'd told her he wasn't Dave Rhodes. She remembered the expression on his face when he'd asked her to stay in Red Bluff. It had been hard for him to ask. Because he had his own fears? The point was that Jase had the courage to face them. Did she?

Thinking about the past year, she realized she'd needed that time to grieve, not only over Dave's death but over her marriage. Apparently she hadn't faced problems between her and Dave or hadn't wanted to see them. They'd never been truly emotionally intimate.

These past few weeks with Jase, on the other hand...

She'd glimpsed real intimacy, real friendship, a real bond that could go deeper than anything she'd ever experienced.

If she had the courage to give him her trust.

She could learn to trust again, couldn't she? She could tell Jase she loved him. She could stay in Red Bluff and try to teach him the power of commitment. Snatching up her keys, she ran for the car.

From listening to the scanner, she knew exactly where the accident had taken place. It wasn't far from Frank's ranch. She pressed her foot to the accelerator, intent on getting there as fast as she could.

It was easy finding the red-and-white flashing lights. She pulled up in back of a police cruiser, hopped out and started running. When she saw Virgil standing at his car with a clipboard, she asked, "Where's Jase?"

"Mrs. Rhodes, you shouldn't be here."

"I'm here, and I want to see Jase. Was he hurt?"

"Not so bad he couldn't round up those burglars all on his own. Apparently they tried to ram him. But he managed to push them off the road before anyone else could get hurt. He had them cuffed and on the ground before Chuck and I got here."

She didn't care about the burglars; she only cared about Jase, and it sounded as if he *had* been hurt. The wail of the ambulance siren got closer and it pulled up in front of the cruiser. She started toward it. Virgil stretched out an arm to grab her before she rushed ahead, but she eluded him, heading for the SUV, which was tilted cockeyed in the ditch, its left front smashed in. The already battered pickup was crinkled on the front right and lodged against a tree. Allison panicked, wondering if Jase was lying on the ground somewhere.

But Virgil had said—

The paramedics rushed toward Chuck and two other officers standing over two cuffed men about ten yards from the SUV.

Then she saw Jase, at the rear of the SUV, talking on his mobile phone.

Running to him, she saw there were cuts on his left cheek and jaw. But he seemed unmindful of them as he switched off the phone, and then saw her.

"You're hurt," she said, worried.

"What are you doing here?" He looked astonished to see her, and not too happy about it, either.

"I had to know you were all right. I heard on the scanner—"

"You shouldn't be here, Allison."

"I had to know that you were all right," she repeated again.

"Why?" he asked gruffly, summing up everything in the question.

There seemed to be noise all around them, and yet the silence and the two feet between them seemed to smother the distraction of everything else.

Now is the time to be courageous, she told herself. *You might never have another chance.*

"Because I love you." Her voice was so low she wondered if he'd heard her. She rushed on, "When I heard your car was involved in an accident, I knew I couldn't go back to Richmond. I know you're telling the truth about your friendship with Maria. I know you're not Dave. I know you're not the kind of man he was. If you tell me I can trust you, Jase, I'll...believe you."

Jase McGraw realized he'd reached a defining moment in his life. Everything he could ever want was in his grasp if he had the courage to say what was in his heart. Maybe if he had said it sooner, Allison's doubts wouldn't have torn her apart—or almost torn them apart. Hearing her words, seeing the love shining in her eyes, he knew that everything they felt between them was stronger than any legacy of his father's. It was stronger than his past. He knew he could be faithful to her because she was the only woman he'd ever truly wanted...or loved.

Setting the phone on the fender of the SUV, he clasped her hands in his. "You *can* trust me, Allison. I promise you that. I'll promise you a lot more if you'll let me. I told you I didn't know if any man could settle down. I think he can when he meets the right woman. I've never been able to settle down. I've never been able to commit myself to anyone because I've always loved you. I don't want anyone else. I don't need anyone else. I never will. Will you marry me?''

She looked stunned, and he supposed he felt a little bit like that himself. But he was sure of what he'd said, and even more sure they could build a life together.

"You love me?" she asked in a very small voice.

Then he knew it was time to show her instead of just tell her, and he slid his hands into her hair, bringing her to him…bringing them together.

She wrapped her arms around him as if she wanted to hold on to him forever. Her kiss was freer than any they'd shared before, and he could feel her desire and her need, as much as he could feel his own. Their lips clung, their tongues danced, their bodies pressed into each other, yearning for a union that would make them one. Jase knew he had to slow it down, knew he had to back off…until they were married. Then he realized she hadn't answered his question yet.

Leaning his forehead against hers, he asked, "*Will* you marry me?"

Her expression was radiant, her cheeks were flushed, her eyes were sparkling, as she smiled and said, "Yes, I'll marry you."

Then he enfolded her in his arms again, not caring about the flashing lights or his deputies keeping watch over the burglars, or the curious but amused stare of the paramedic who was now standing at his elbow. "Sheriff McGraw, I just came over to check you out."

Lifting his head, Jase grinned at him. "Don't worry

about me. I've never felt better.'' Then he bent to Allison, to kiss her again…to show everyone who wanted to see that he'd found the love of his life, and he was never going to let her go.

Epilogue

The cooler October temperatures were bringing lots of changes into their lives, Allison thought, as she opened the door to their new house, a department store bag in each hand.

Jase was removing leather-bound books from a carton and sliding them onto the oak bookshelves that lined one wall of the living room between two windows. She loved their new house, situated on a piece of land Frank had sold Jase. But she loved her husband of two years even more. Over and over she'd discovered that Jase had an old-fashioned streak. If they had a daughter...

She smiled, thinking about the pregnancy test she'd bought and used this morning, thinking about the life growing inside of her. She'd wanted to be sure, because she didn't know exactly what Jase's reaction would be. They'd decided they'd let nature take its course, but the actuality of a baby arriving in eight months was different than just the possibility.

"I think these shelves are going to be filled with the rest of the books your parents brought out last month." Jase turned from the shelves and smiled at her, the slow, welcoming smile that told her this was exactly where she belonged.

"I bought appliance covers for the toaster and mixer, and a few other things." She hadn't been able to resist a pair of baby booties and a small stuffed lamb.

Coming over to her, he took the bags from her hands and laid them on the sofa. Then he slipped his arms around her waist. "I missed you when I got home."

"You must have gotten home early."

"Since I worked late last night, I figured I could get the unpacking done today. Then we could stop tripping over boxes, and maybe have some fun in bed."

She loved that about him. He was always straightforward with her, telling her exactly what he wanted. She tried to be that way with him. After he'd asked her to marry him, he'd told her straight out he didn't want her to have any doubts, and they were going to do things properly. The next day, he'd taken her to buy an engagement ring, and then they'd planned their wedding for three months later. Even though he'd moved her into a rooming house for propriety's sake, they'd spent as much time together as they could manage for those three months. There was never any doubt that they were meant for each other, never any doubt that she should meld her life with his.

It had been frustrating for them both to wait until their wedding night to make love, but they had. Jase had insisted on it. That old-fashioned streak emerging again.

Now she kissed him, telling him she was glad she was home...telling him she was grateful he was her husband...telling him she loved the life they led together that was going to get even better.

He broke away to murmur, "Let's take this into the bedroom."

"I'd like to show you what I bought first."

He raised his head, looking surprised. "These appliance covers better be pretty special."

She laughed, suddenly nervous.

While she retrieved the bag from the sofa, he said, "I've been thinking. When you get your nurse practitioner's license in January, we should have a really big party and celebrate. Maybe we can even talk your folks into coming out."

Allison's parents had known *of* Jase for years, but had never really known him. After she called them to tell them she was engaged, they'd come out for a visit. It had been awkward at first, but then Jase had taken her parents to the bluff where he'd shown her the first New Mexican sunset. They'd gone sightseeing in Albuquerque. They'd sat and talked on the patio many nights, and her parents had soon realized she was happier than she'd ever been before, and that Jase was a good man.

Bringing the bag over to him, she said, "Maybe we should just wait and have the party for another occasion."

"What occasion would that be?"

Opening the bag, she took out the small cuddly lamb and the pair of yellow baby booties.

He gazed deep into her eyes, then swung her up into his arms, lamb and booties, too. "You're pregnant?"

"It seems that way. I took a pregnancy test this morning. I guess I could take another one—"

He cut her off with a deep, lasting kiss, that would have made her crumple to the floor if he hadn't been holding her in his arms. Then he carried her toward their bedroom.

As she held on to the lamb, she asked, "I guess you're happy about this?"

"I'm going to show you exactly *how* happy."

"I can't wait," she said breathlessly. Jase was her world, and her love, and her life. And now, with the baby—

When he took her into their bedroom, he laid her gently on the bed, and then came down beside her. "Do you know how happy you've made me?"

She nodded. "As happy as *you've* made *me*."

Smiling, she reached for him, and he reached for her. Desire wrapped in love overtook them—as it had before—as it would again—and they renewed their vows, professed their love, and rejoiced over the new life growing within her. She and Jase would be friends, lovers, partners and now parents, for the rest of their lives.

When he made her his, she held on to him and he held on to her. She was his lady and he was her lawman.

Until the end of time.

*   *   *   *   *

*Be sure to look for the next book from
Karen Rose Smith, HER TYCOON BOSS,
available in June 2001
from Silhouette Romance.*

**Don't miss the reprisal of
Silhouette Romance's popular miniseries**

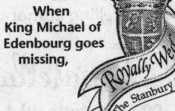

When
King Michael of
Edenbourg goes
missing,

his devoted
family and loyal
subjects make it
their mission to bring
him home safely!

**Their search begins March 2001 and
continues through June 2001.**

On sale March 2001: **THE EXPECTANT PRINCESS**
by bestselling author **Stella Bagwell** (SR #1504)

On sale April 2001: **THE BLACKSHEEP PRINCE'S BRIDE**
by rising star **Martha Shields** (SR #1510)

On sale May 2001: **CODE NAME: PRINCE**
by popular author **Valerie Parv** (SR #1516)

On sale June 2001: **AN OFFICER AND A PRINCESS**
by award-winning author **Carla Cassidy** (SR #1522)

Available at your favorite retail outlet.

Where love comes alive™

**Join Silhouette Books as
award-winning, bestselling author**

Marie Ferrarella

celebrates her 100th Silhouette title!

Don't miss
ROUGH AROUND THE EDGES
Silhouette Romance #1505
March 2001

To remain in the United States, Shawn O'Rourke
needed a wife. Kitt Dawson needed a home
for herself and the baby daughter Shawn
had helped her deliver. A marriage of
convenience seemed the perfect solution—
until they discovered that the real thing was
much more appealing than playacting....

Available at your favorite retail outlet.

Where love comes alive™

Silhouette —

where love comes alive—online...

eHARLEQUIN.com

your romantic life

—Romance 101—
♥ Guides to romance, dating and flirting.

—Dr. Romance —
♥ Get romance advice and tips from our expert, Dr. Romance.

—Recipes for Romance—

♥ How to plan romantic meals for you and your sweetie.

—Daily Love Dose—
♥ Tips on how to keep the romance alive every day.

—Tales from the Heart—
♥ Discuss romantic dilemmas with other members in our Tales from the Heart message board.